Albatross

By Ross Turner

Pammy-sue,

Congratulations!

Thank you for entering.

Enjoy!

Ross/

Ross Turner

©Ross Turner

Albatross

Family can mean lots of different things,
It doesn't have to be blood,
It can be whatever we make of it,

Here's to a new life,

And perhaps one day, if I am very fortunate, I shall come to know my place in this world,

Always,

Ross.

Contents

1. Uprooted
2. Keepers Cottage
3. The Rusty Oak
4. Skylight Nights on Sea View Side
5. She Who Interferes
6. Deacon
7. Memoria Lane
8. Sunlit Chorus
9. Lust
10. Anticipation
11. On Top of the World
12. The Façade
13. Dyra's Warning
14. HOME
15. The Grotto
16. Elusive Desert Islands
17. Lost in You, Again
18. Around Your Neck
19. Breaching Barriers

20. Hard Truths
21. Lagoon of Excuses
22. Dancing with the Devil
23. Greenway
24. The Artist and the Impersonator
25. Unforeseen Shadows
26. Predator and Prey
27. Decisions
28. Truth
29. Revelations
30. Letting Go

Uprooted

Jen had moved house so many times over the last decade, and her little family had been uprooted so frequently, that she barely knew if she was coming or going anymore. Quite often, when she sat with herself, she tried to think back and name all the places she had lived, but hard as she tried, she rarely ever managed even half of them.

All the different towns and cities they had explored, and all the multitudes of street names and house numbers they had lived at, seemed most of the time lost on her. Not that Jen really saw it as a problem, as they rarely stayed in the same place for more than a few months at a time, so though she often thought back, she never really let it bother her.

Currently she found herself sat cross legged upon a rocky outcrop, and though she had found as comfortable a spot as she could, the ground was hard and unforgiving beneath her.

Her ragged, dark brown hair whipped about her fair face and over her shoulders in the fierce wind, while her eyes, the same deep chocolate colour to match, scanned the horizon for as far as she could see.

Blue jeans, torn here and there, out of use rather than style, scuffed white trainers, and a well-worn, plain black hoody, was all that the young lady of a mere nineteen years old wore. And she was comfortable, not really worrying about fashion or dressing to impress.

Albatross

Her hoody kept the chill wind at bay, and her trainers were better on the rocks than the kinds of shoes most people wore. And since she came out here quite often, enjoying the rocks and the waves and the solitude of her own company, it just made sense to her.

In fact, considering the sheer amount of time she spent on the beach, had there been a house, a cottage, or even a shack, built upon the sands, she would quite happily have inhabited it. Quite often she imagined such a thing, but as with everything else, wondering notions were all it would ever remain.

The rocks were jagged and dangerous and seethed here and there. Every now and then the freezing cold water of the North Atlantic Ocean rose and swelled and battered their exposed faces, spraying and foaming as harshly and as often as possible.

White water rushed and swirled between the huge boulders, widening splits and cracks over the years and eddying its way as far up the beach as possible, though knowing without a shadow of a doubt that there would never be a way to truly escape.

Even through her thick hoody Jen could feel the cold, and the temperature seemed to drop dramatically and seep through to her very bones.

She shuddered suddenly and sighed, glancing down at her hands in her lap, feeling decidedly melancholy.

Looking up again and out into the distance Jen counted four boats on the far horizon, stretched out across the ocean before her. Two were massive tankers that looked tiny and insignificant from so far away, but she imagined were so enormous it would have taken her days to explore them. One looked like a yacht of some description, though it was hard to tell from where she sat. And the fourth, the furthest of the lot, was so far out on the horizon that it was barely even a spec, and she couldn't make out its outline at all.

To her left, as she looked across and the wind lashed at her exposed face, was a wide, arcing bay lined with strips of sand that ran in parallel rows all along the beach front, and between her and the sand sat hundreds upon hundreds of rocks, each bigger and more jagged and more brooding than the last.

Two huge columns protruded up higher than all of the others. One reached about five or six metres above the level of the water thrashing around its base, and the other reached more like ten or twelve, and both were sheer and vertical on all sides.

A few hardy, or perhaps misguided souls were attempting to jump across to the columns and climb them before the next wave came crashing in and swept them away. They were all soaked though, so clearly they had not been too successful, but they kept trying nonetheless.

Even in the twelve months or so, just over, that she had lived here, which was truly something of a record for her family, Jen had seen many a time the lifeboat crews trying in vain to rescue people cast against the harsh rocks by the rough ocean.

The waters here, in lieu with the unpredictable weather, made for a treacherous Welsh coastline.

It had been only a few weeks ago in fact that, exploring too close to the edge, as children do, a young boy was swept from the safety of the pier and cast down into the seething waters by a huge wave on a particularly high tide.

A full three days it took for his body to be found.

His family were devastated.

Jen shook her head as if trying to scare away her thoughts.

This most certainly wasn't helping her mood, and she tried desperately to focus on something else.

Quite often she tried that, however, and not once yet to any avail.

To her right the rocks turned to sand and the beach stretched out long and thin along the coastline straight ahead, which eventually met more rocks in the far distance.

Laid out alongside the sand was a beach of pebbles, and then behind the pebbles a path that ran the entire length of the coast, disappearing in the distance as it veered right and round the corner.

A few figures dotted along the path made their way to a fro. Some were alone and watched as their dogs chased seagulls along the beach, barking with delight as the gulls cawed in annoyance.

Closest to her, Jen saw a small family making their way along the path in her direction. The mother and father walked hand in hand and pointed something out along the horizon to their youngest daughter, whilst their elder daughter skipped ahead slightly.

She was still only about ten years of age, and carried a stuffed giraffe under one arm. Jen could only presume she had won it at the fair, up and round to the right, along in the next bay, where the path disappeared to.

The family soon passed by however, and by now, having been sat for quite some time, the cold was beginning to creep its way into Jen's very core, and she decided it was time to make a move.

Her legs groaned and ached as she uncrossed them and pushed herself to stand, but she forced them to move, knowing they would loosen off soon enough.

As she rose the wind caught her off guard and almost knocked her off balance, but she had spent many long days on these rocks and she found her footing soon enough, steadying herself between two protruding boulders cast off at treacherous angles.

Beginning at a walk, but soon breaking into a run, Jen hopped along the rocks, jagged and dangerous and uneven, moving faster and faster by the second. Her expression was grim, but her eyes darted everywhere, looking for safe places to put her feet.

Her legs moved and churned somehow even faster than her tumbling thoughts, finding sometimes not so sure footing, but always somehow just enough to keep her from falling.

Rising high and then dipping down low, Jen wove her way along the crags that lined the bay.

When she dropped low the waves crashed in and threatened to sweep her away, swelling through cracks and creating maelstroms in huge potholes. They washed crabs in and out of rock pools and spewed foam and harsh sea spray as far as possible over the dry, grey faces of the rocks, sat so ominously above.

Occasionally Jen got caught in the spray, but before long, feeling gloomy still, she decided that it wasn't enough to get caught just on the edge of danger, but instead that she needed to be right in the thick of it, amidst the water and the waves themselves.

The feeling that drove her in that moment was a strange one indeed, somehow combining self-destruction and self-preservation all into one. Jen dropped down right into the path of the deafening waves, only darting out of the way right at the last moment.

Sometimes though, she didn't quite make it in time, and her one foot or leg got engulfed and soaked.

There was one moment even, in an instant of hesitation, when both of her legs were very nearly swept from beneath her. But she wasn't quite pulled in, managing to scrape her way back up the rocks at the last moment, though only by the skin of her teeth.

Eventually, when that particularly big wave caught her off guard, soaking her completely up to her waist, turning her jeans a very dark blue, Jen retreated back amongst the higher rocks for safety.

She wandered off slowly towards the sand, her feet squelching unpleasantly in her sodden shoes, and the cold wind now seeming to cut straight through her wet clothes, making her shudder violently and her teeth chatter uncontrollably.

Heavy clouds swarmed above and perched threateningly on the skyline. There was no warmth from the sun today able to penetrate the thick grey barrier above her, and Jen pulled her hoody ever more tightly up around her neck.

Dropping her gaze from the sky to the ground, Jen sighed again. The rocks were a dull, vicious grey.

As ever.

The water itself had no colour to it and looked exhausted and bleak, and even the sand upon which she now walked looked devoid of all life and colour.

It was as if the very soul had been drained from the coast and the water lapped up the grim sand laboriously, with the weight of the world bearing down upon it.

The only colour all around came from the gulls that cawed and squawked in their shrill, high pitched cries that always seemed startled and craving and devious all at once.

They dove down to surprise unsuspecting beach wanderers at every opportunity, stealing much of their food in the process. Chips, fish, and even whole pies were amongst the wreckage as the devilish birds sent them cascading across the sand and the rocks, only then to immediately swarm upon them with what seemed like a hundred hoarding comrades.

Jen watched the carnage for a few minutes as the gulls put into practice their perfectly honed skills, dispatching three or four meals with relative ease.

But then, suddenly, amidst the chaos, the gulls screamed and shrieked and scattered as if a crazed wolf had been thrown amongst the sheep.

As they leapt into the sky and battered their wings desperately against the wind, a single, much larger, much more menacing figure became clear amidst the squawking masses.

Albatross

Peering as best she could between the frantically flurrying crowds of beating wings, jerking and spiralling in every direction, Jen couldn't help but search for the creature that she had glimpsed, drawn to it, fixated by it.

Finally the rabble cleared, and Jen straightened up to look at the creature straight on, and in turn, it looked back at her, blinking slowly and cocking its head slightly to one side, thinking.

It was another bird.

At first she thought it was just a big gull.

But as she looked on at it, Jen realised that she was mistaken.

Its long yellow beak was tipped with vibrant orange, contrasting everything around it so obviously that the colour sang like a siren and flashed like a beacon.

Set deep into its face and jet black as coal, its eyes looked most serious as they surveyed their surroundings, touched with much more than just a hint of sadness.

Compared to the rest of the gulls, this bird had an enormous wingspan. Jen's eyes must have been playing tricks on her, because she could have sworn that as it stretched out, the incredible bird was almost the size of a fully grown man.

But nonetheless, as it stretched, Jen couldn't help but take in every detail of the magnificent creature.

The underside of its wings were perfect white, shaded only on their very edges with jet black, whilst their topside was coloured entirely, like its eyes.

It ignored the food strewn about by the gulls' raiding attacks, as if it were not important in the slightest; as if it knew that such ridiculous and petty thievery was something only they should participate in. It took three or four slow and purposeful steps towards Jen, eyeing her cautiously, but inquisitively.

The seagulls were like rats with wings.

Flying vermin.

This was something altogether and entirely different.

Still, Jen didn't know what this creature was, but she knew at least that it was no ordinary gull.

That much was plain to see.

"That's an albatross." Clare said suddenly then, shattering the silence like a foghorn, warning of danger.

Clare was Jen's sister: her non identical twin sister, to be exact.

She had been there the whole time.

She always was.

Jen looked over to Clare curiously. Her eyes and hair were dark also, like hers, though much thicker and much more lustrous, and although they looked similar, they were quite clearly, at the same time, very different.

Clare's skin was much fuller, and her frame more curvy and feminine and attractive, whilst Jen's seemed weakened by something that long sapped at the strength and the soul.

And while behind Jen's eyes there was a deep rooted sadness, there was nothing of the sort behind Clare's, and her gaze was filled with such life and love that it seemed quite incredulous.

Albatross

"It can't be…?" Jen questioned, furrowing her brow and glancing briefly between the glorious bird and her older sister.

"It is, Jenny." Clare replied confidently, and Jen was instantly convinced.

"How do you know?" Jen asked her sister then, looking across again at Clare, stood a ways away on the dull grey sand.

Even just stood there, against the dreary backdrop, Clare looked more vibrant and full of life than Jen could ever possibly hope to be. But it didn't bring her down in the slightest. In fact, Jen didn't even really notice.

The albatross looked up at them both and its gaze seemed somehow knowing, and even more saddened than before, as if it saw some terrible truth that they could not.

Jen was confused by the sight, and frowned again slightly, deep in thought.

She glanced over to her sister once more, but Clare's expression was much more understanding, and agreeing even, as if she somehow knew exactly what the beautiful, enormous creature was thinking.

Jen didn't ask however, and deliberately so, for some reason, entirely and purposefully ignoring what had seemed to pass between Clare and the albatross.

Then, since he saw that Jen was going to intentionally ignore what he was trying to tell her, the albatross sighed sorrowfully and regretfully, if that were even possible, and spread his vast wings as wide as they would go.

With only the slightest of movements, he caught the snapping breeze and lifted his perfect white body, outstanding so clearly against the greyness all around, effortlessly ascending into the air.

Watching as in seemingly seconds the albatross disappeared off into the distance, carried at terrifying speed by the wind, Jen felt as though she should have listened.

But still, knowing what she would hear, she firmly refused to do so.

She looked across to Clare, asking for forgiveness merely with her gaze, and of course her sister gave it to her, though she had a strange, whimsical look painted across her face.

They watched the magical bird disappear towards the horizon, far in the distance. The line dividing the sea and the sky was barely even visible as the grey of the water and the grey of the dim skies merged together, virtually into one.

Jen felt a strange connection to the mysterious creature as it floated away, alone, lost in this bleak, solitary place.

The only real difference between them, she thought in that moment, was that she could not simply spread her wings and fly away, and escape from all of this. And all of a sudden, overwhelmed by grief, young Jen Williams longed for nothing more than that: to merely spread her wings and vanish into the distance.

Keepers Cottage

"An albatross?" Dyra asked, her tone disbelieving. "Are you sure, Jennifer?"

"Yes mom!" Jen replied almost absently as she frantically searched online through thousands of pictures of different birds, looking for the closest image to the one she had seen.

"How do you know?" Her mother asked then.

Dyra's hair was long and dark, as were her eyes, but her gaze was not touched with flashes of grey in the way her hair was. She looked so much like her two daughters that it was quite uncanny, and the pictures of the three of them that were dotted all about the house showed that quite evidently.

"Clare told me." Jen replied automatically, as if her older sister's word was gospel. "She was sure of it."

"Jennifer…" Her mother exhaled then, her spirit drowning suddenly, but her youngest daughter interrupted her before she could finish.

"Please, don't call me that, mom…" Jen asked on a whim, still frantically scrolling through webpages and search engines, looking for the perfect picture to match what she had seen. "You're the only one that calls me Jennifer…" She continued absently. "Everyone else calls me Jen. Except Clare. She calls me Jenny…"

Dyra sighed deeply, giving up on what she was saying before she'd even begun.

She knew her daughter wouldn't hear her.

Not yet.

Though from the outside their home looked like rather an old building, verging almost even on an archaic cottage, Dyra much preferred to refer to it as antique, rather than old, and besides, on the inside it was quite different.

Wooden beams that supported the ceiling were cut perfectly square and with a modern, polished finish. The surfaces were marble and cut smooth and precisely, dark and grey and set upon solid oak cupboards and worktops.

The table at which Jen sat in the kitchen, fingers tapping the laptop in a frenzy, was a heavy, dark oak; very old, but in immaculate condition. Aside from the table, the kitchen was modernised and orderly, with utensils all either tidied away into draws, or sat upright in labelled, metal pots.

There were white, crock pots of tea and coffee and sugar too, all lined up in neat rows along the counter, and each container had inscribed upon it the contents in thick, black letters.

In the living room, just across the hallway, with the front door on one side and the stairs on the other, statues and ornaments were scattered around of all sorts of different animals and figures.

There were miniature wooden giraffes and elephants that marched across sideboards, and even a small ceramic Buddha that perched above the wood burning fireplace, set back a ways beneath the chimney breast and plated with highly polished steel.

Also, regardless of what room you were in, the walls were lined with pictures and memories, and the sideboards scattered intermittently between the herds with upright frames.

Mostly they were pictures of Jen and Clare, the two of them so similar. And then, here and there, you would see a picture of all three of them: Jen, Clare, and their mother, Dyra.

Some were small and just taken on a whim, in a back garden or out for the evening. Whilst others, much larger and more prominent, had been taken at more momentous occasions.

The day they'd moved in here, for example, just over a year ago, was one such occasion. They had planned to stay here indefinitely, and that picture of the three of them, stood in front of the cottage, had pride and place up on the stairwell.

Another was the picture of the three of them at the lake they'd visited at the end of the summer, only just after they'd moved in. They'd managed to catch a warm, sunny day towards the end of September, and spent it messing around and having fun on the water; a day that was one of their fondest memories.

As for the cottage itself, the front of the house faced inland, opening out past their narrow front garden onto Shortberry Lane, while the back of the house faced the shoreline, not really all that far in the distance.

"Here! This one!" Jen suddenly exclaimed.

Her mother didn't really like to humour this; Jennifer had promised her after all.

However, this was the most excited she'd seen her youngest daughter in a long while: weeks, months, probably even the whole year.

Perhaps it was a turning point.

She turned to look at the image Jen had pulled up and enlarged on the screen of the laptop.

"Is that what you saw?" Dyra asked, her voice laced intricately with dubiousness.

The picture Jennifer was showing her was indeed an albatross. Its long yellow beak was tipped with orange so bright that it was practically luminous, and its wingspan was impressive to the point of being excessive.

It was indeed a magnificent creature, but not the sort of animal that regularly patrolled the Welsh coastline.

"Yes!" Jen replied, absolutely certain. "That exactly!"

"I've never seen anything like that…" Her mother, Dyra, commented. "How did Clare know what it was?" She asked, her tone shifting slightly as she swallowed hard.

But Jen only shrugged.

Scrolling through the endless reams of information on the screen, pages and pages flitted by much too quickly for Dyra to keep up with, and Jen's eyes darted left and right and up and down as she read.

"It must be here somewhere…" She muttered to herself as she scrolled.

By this point Dyra was lost amidst the infinite webpages and paragraphs. She had never really got on with computers.

She much preferred a book to a screen.

Dyra stood up for a moment and sighed, pursing her lips mournfully and resting her hands on her hips.

"Ah!" Jen suddenly cried, apparently having found what she had been looking for.

"What is it?" Dyra asked, but almost even before she could speak Jen began reading from the screen.

"They range widely in the Southern Ocean and North Pacific…" She recited. "But are absent from the North Atlantic…"

Jen paused then and her brow furrowed in thought, confused. She read on silently, her eyes flitting at an unbelievable speed. Then she checked and double checked that she hadn't missed anything, before finally conceding.

It seemed, according to this at least, that there were no exceptions.

There should not be any albatross here.

"Where is your sister anyway?" Dyra asked suddenly then, seeming to change the subject entirely. Jen's mother glanced round briefly as she spoke, though for no real reason in particular.

"She's gone out to work, mom…" Jen replied absently, stealing a quick glance out of the window at the slowly darkening sky as if that had been obvious.

"Oh, right…" Dyra replied then, her tone dropping again. "Of course…" She moved away from the computer and returned to tending distractedly to the cleaning of worktops in the kitchen.

Jen filched another glance from the computer screen, except this time it was to follow her mother's movements from across the room with a steely gaze, as she nipped through into the living room.

"Do you have work tonight, honey?" Dyra called back through after a few moments.

"Yeah. I'm going in a minute." Jen replied, her tone very level.

She dragged her chair slowly back and the legs scraped loudly on the tile floor. Rising to her feet, in a flurry of movement Jen closed all that she had been looking at on the laptop and darted from her seat.

"Oh, right…" Dyra started, ceasing her cleaning and stepping back through to the kitchen at the sound of Jen's sudden haste. "It's just that Mandy said she wanted to pop in to see you today…"

"Oh…" Her daughter uttered. "Sorry, I've got to go now…" Jen apologised, though by her tone it was obvious that the idea of a visit from Mandy was not something that overly enthralled her.

"Ok sweetheart, don't worry." Her mother replied with a slight smile, kind and understanding, as mothers are supposed to be. "I'll phone her and ask her to come another day."

"Thank you mom." Jen replied simply, returning the smile and hugging Dyra quickly before rummaging beneath the table for her rucksack.

Within barely minutes Jen had collected all of her things for work, which consisted really of little more than a jacket and some morsels of food, and she was on her way out of the door.

"I'll be back later mom!" The young girl called over her shoulder as she pulled the front door open, painted a thick, rich red colour, a door handle and letterbox set in its very centre, one above the other.

And then above the both of them, hung upon a rusty nail, driven into the wooden face of the door, was a sign scrawled upon with fine black paint.

Keepers Cottage

"Be careful please!" Dyra called back automatically.

"Don't worry!" Jen replied as she pulled the door to behind her. "I'm meeting Clare after work! We'll walk home together!"

And with that Jen was gone.

She closed the door behind her and it clicked firmly into place. She was soon down the short garden path, crossing the evenly set stones ditched into the grass on slightly uneven angles, framed by flowers on either side, and out onto Shortberry Lane.

Her mother, Dyra, remained, standing alone in the hallway, looking longingly after her youngest daughter.

Her arms hung limply at her sides, her one hand clutching a rag, and thick tears stood heavily in her eyes, as they often did nowadays.

The Rusty Oak

The day darkened more quickly as Jen walked briskly down the winding lanes towards The Rusty Oak.

The lanes were narrow, in quite a few places wide enough for only one car to pass, and frequently drivers trying to come through were forced to reverse up to a crossing place to allow others to get by.

Jen knew these roads in and out by now though, even after just barely twelve months of living here, and she regularly cut through the bush here and there to miss out the biggest loops in the winding tongue of tarmac that sliced so abhorrently through the countryside. She saved an awful lot of time in the process, and a journey that would have taken her nearly an hour, had she stuck to the roads, took her barely half that time nipping through the undergrowth.

Sometimes though, after heavy downpours in the colder, wetter months, the months that were so rapidly encroaching now, her shortcuts were simply too wet and too boggy to be of any use whatsoever, and she was forced to stick to the road.

Passing by houses and cottages as she walked, more often than not named instead of numbered, like their own, Jen glanced quickly over at each of them in turn.

The names varied greatly, and some were original and quirky, whilst others were most definitely not.

The Old Police House

It was a long, low building with many thin, evenly set windows. The roof was made of black, steeply slanted tile, overlapping the walls so that rainfall ran straight to the ground. Hung between each of the ground floor windows was a lantern framed by iron and glass.

In years gone by the lanterns had been filled with oil and lit, but now they served merely as ornaments and reminders of years gone by.

As so many things do.

Next, hidden between the trees to her left, still just about visible in the dimming light, Jen knew which one was coming up.

Thatcher's Retreat

Easily Jen's favourite, this cottage was well hidden away behind the greenery and, as the name suggested, was one of the only remaining houses in the area that still had a genuine thatched roof.

The rest of the cottage was relatively unremarkable, to be honest, but it was its quaint nature that Jen loved so, and its ability to be so unique, and yet so unknown, all at once.

A plain wooden door, cracked and split here and there, faced out between the trees, and marked the entrance to the Thatcher's Retreat. Two square windows sat either side, flickering dimly from within: short, squat, and entirely content with themselves.

There were many more houses and cottages and retreats of all shapes and sizes and designs that Jen knew of, for the most part, off by heart, but the cold was getting to her now as the temperature dropped. The chill bit at her considerably and she slung her rucksack round onto one shoulder and pulled a different hoody from within it.
This one zipped up the front and she pulled it on hastily and did it all the way up to her chin. It was a deep burgundy colour, though it was old and ragged, and she buried her hands in the pockets on its front, rubbing them against the soft material to fight off the cold.
She was nearly there anyway.
All of a sudden, hearing a low, clunking rumble approaching behind her, Jen turned to look, only to be blinded by a set of ridiculously bright headlights, pointing off in slightly skewed directions. Forced to shield her eyes from the beams, she moved off to the side of the road and, as the car's horn honked, strained her eyes, squinting, to see who it was.

Tensing up, her breath caught in her throat and she slunk slowly towards the shadows, gripped by fear.

Her mind screamed at her to run, but even as she reached the shadow of the nearest treeline, she found that as the car pulled closer, she could no longer move. Her body froze in terror, and her legs remained rooted to the ground.

Albatross

Then, once the car came into view more clearly, the rust spots upon the matt black bonnet became clear, and the extremely faded red paint that covered the rest of the car, looking pinkish in the poor light, were a dead giveaway.

She recognised it.

It was one of the chefs she worked with.

"Jen!" A gruff voice called from the grubby driver's window, wound halfway down.

"Hello Geoff." She replied meekly, trying to regain her breath and her composure, greeting the portly, greying chap grinning at her through the murky glass of his windscreen.

"Need a lift?" He asked her, jabbing one fat thumb towards the passenger seat in a lazy gesture. He revved his engine as he did so, though it sounded less like a car and more like a rickety old microwave, years past due replacing.

"Thanks." Jen replied, sidling round the front of the death trap of a car, opening the passenger door and sliding in beside her most definitely oversized colleague.

He was already in his chef whites and, not surprisingly, they were already spotted here and there. They were perhaps tighter than they should have been too, but that didn't appear to be because they were too small, but instead rather because he was too large. Though, of course, Jen never mentioned that observation.

It was, perchance, an occupational hazard, and oddly enough perhaps one that inspired trust in his ability above all else.

Regardless, Geoff was a lovely man and always very friendly.

He wouldn't hurt a fly.

"Good day?" He asked then, as if on cue, grinding and churning his poor car back into first gear as he spoke.

"Yes, thank you." Jen replied, though still a little meekly. "You?"

"Awful!" He declared quite refreshingly, and with a seemingly misplaced laugh as the car lurched forward. He forced it almost immediately into second gear and it groaned and chugged despairingly.

The almost imperceptible sidelong glance that he cast his young colleague, however, betrayed the fact that he'd noticed her immediate withdrawal.

It was nothing new.

Nonetheless, he changed tact slightly.

"How's your mother?" He asked then, pausing for a moment on his words, as if he'd wanted to say more.

"Fine, thank you." Jen replied.

"And Clare?" Geoff asked then.

"Very well, thank you." Jen responded, her mood shifting instantly.

She seemed to rise several feet in her seat as she exploded from her shell and drew a deep breath.

"You'll never guess what we saw at the beach today!" She blurted unexpectedly, enthusiasm suddenly oozing from her every pore, infecting the air all around her.

Geoff smiled, though the bright look in his eyes was dampened somewhat.

"What did you see?" He asked.

Albatross

And though his eyes betrayed his true feelings, it was too dark for Jen to see them; his tone did not reveal a thing, and he matched her enthusiasm almost exactly.

He had always been very good at reading people.

To him, Jen was easy to read, but recently a lot of people had strayed from her, and more and more often he had found her confiding in him in many subtle little ways.

This was just yet another example.

"We saw an albatross!" She exclaimed, gesturing with her hands across the dashboard. "It was huge!"

"What!?" Geoff replied, shocked, gripped now with genuine curiosity. "Really!?"

"Really!" Jen confirmed, opening up much more now. "I didn't know what it was at first. It was Clare that knew it was an albatross!"

"How did she know?" Geoff asked carefully then.

"You know how smart she's always been!" Jen declared, as if that explained everything. "I just can't believe we saw it!"

"I know…" Geoff agreed. "I've never heard of such a thing here in my life…" He continued, but hard as he tried, his tone dropped noticeably with his words.

Jen sensed his hesitance, knowing exactly what he was thinking, and within seconds she felt her deep set melancholy returning.

The car clunked on and the gears ground continuously as they drove, now the only noise besides the occasional barking in the distance that could be heard over the trees.

Not a moment too soon The Rusty Oak came into view, illuminated amidst the darkness in a way that always seemed so inviting. The base of its triangular, slated roof faced the road upon approach, and was lined with yellow fairy lights, and on each corner a spotlight cast light like moonbeams across the entrance and front terrace.

Geoff ground his car to a juddering halt, but before it had even come to a complete stop, Jen was out of the door.

"Thanks Geoff…" She called quietly to him as she stepped out and closed the door gently behind her, making immediately for the wooden doors filled with coloured glass set above a single black, metal letterbox. Even upon brief first glance it was clear that inside the pub it was already busy, but even so, Geoff paused for a moment before he got out.

Sighing deeply, he sat back and ran his shovel like hands through his greying hair, receding on both sides. He watched Jen disappear inside, slipping through the doors like a ghost, and a sullen mixture of sorrow, regret and pity swelled inside of him, as he thought on what he saw.

Perhaps the best phrase to describe The Rusty Oak, above all others, would have been old fashioned. And in turn, undoubtedly the best word to describe it, would have been rustic.

The pub's history was very English, and naturally, in turn, very cruel and very sad.

Albatross

At the back of the large building, constructed itself from huge blocks all painted white, set here and there with square, wooden framed windows, and capped with a slate roof, lay varnished decking that stretched out for almost two dozen feet. Ideal for summer's evenings spent with friends and family, sipping cold drinks and watching life go by.

However, beyond the decking, set apart from everything else, stood the single figure of an enormous oak tree; solitary and timeless.

Where once the tree had been made of bark and branches and leaves and the very essence of life itself, now, instead, the tree that stood in its place was made of iron, pulled reluctantly from the earth and bent to the will of man.

Over time the iron had rusted, as is its nature, and the tree that stood there now was a strange mixture of black and grey and red and copper, all at once.

Once upon a time, on this very spot, just as they still did to this day, friends and family had indeed flocked here on warm summer's evenings, sipped cold drinks and laughed and joked, as a bear was tied to the tree and baited with savage dogs.

Always, inhumane bloodlust ensued.

But the cruelty of entertainment such as this is sadly all too often lost on most people, for we are indeed a violent and primitive race.

Either the bear would claim victory, killing every animal the handlers could throw at it, and live to fight another day, only to be carted away to the next inn to suffer the same fate. Or, the poor beast would succumb, overwhelmed by numbers and a lifetime of injuries and suffering, as is more often than not the case, in many more ways than just one.

Naturally, the baiters would do their best to avoid the latter. Their livelihoods, and indeed the lives of their families, oddly enough, depended on the bear, and they needed it to suffer for as long as physically possible for the amusement of man.

One day though, or so the story goes, enraged so by the dogs attacking it, the bear rose to its full, terrifying height, and roared with dreadful anger and sadness, much to the delight of the inn's onlookers.

But then, to everyone's disbelief, and shortly after, terror, the poor monster hauled forward with all its might and ripped the vast oak tree from the very ground, roots and all.

Charging blindly and unstoppably, the frightened beast pummelled three massive dogs into the dirt, and promptly ate its handlers.

Now, whether a little, or perchance a lot, of artistic license was employed in the embellishment of that story, perhaps we'll never know. But, nonetheless, the oak tree was replaced with an identical iron one, in memory of the poor brute, which, incidentally, or so the story goes, was stoned to death shortly afterwards.

Hopefully needless to say, bears were never baited at The Rusty Oak again.

Immediately Geoff was busy, dashing here and there, his giant hands working in a frenzy and his step seemingly far too quick for a man of his generous dimensions. There was little time to talk as orders rushed in constantly, but the more orders that came in, the faster Geoff seemed to move, feeding off the relentless pace endlessly.

He loved it, smiling and humming to himself as he worked.

Jen too moved quickly, flitting about as she always seemed to in the bustling kitchen.

Like a ghost.

Like she wasn't even there.

And, since it seems to be the time for stories of the past, she too once upon a time used to smile and hum as she worked. On occasion even, on days when humming simply wasn't enough, she used to sing too.

But of late, her love of singing, and of cooking, of everything in fact, it seemed, had vanished.

Geoff had watched this decline with sorrow in his heart. As he had witnessed only that evening, in their short car journey to the pub, there was only one thing that seemed to stir any kind of emotion in Jen nowadays.

And that was her dear sister, Clare.

He frequently glanced across at her as she prepped meals and desserts for him in a robotic, melancholy state.

Yet again he sighed, not knowing what could be done.

Waiters and waitresses dipped in and out throughout the night and Jen and Geoff waltzed round the kitchen together, dipping and weaving between fridges and ovens and pots and pans in an intricate dance. There was a rhythmical perfection to their harmony, and even a comedic element about it, as the overly large chef and the, in comparison, seemingly undersized young girl, worked flawlessly together. They'd had plenty of practice after all.

Again, it was something Jen had used to love, and they had laughed many nights of work away in their comical routine.

Used to love.

The whole situation saddened Geoff greatly.

There was a new lad who had recently started, who often appeared looking more than a little overwhelmed, but Jen had cocooned herself so much that she didn't even know his name.

She did however, know Laura.

Laura Patterson.

Businesswoman.

Owner of The Rusty Oak.

Having spent years helping her father run the pub, for it had been in their family for more than a few generations, Laura treated The Rusty Oak as if it were an only child.

She was caring and friendly and gave everybody anything she could, but the second anybody started to get rowdy, she came down on them in a heartbeat.

It worked very well, and she was very good at it. Though she was only slight, and not overly tall, her voice could be both kind and stern, and her light hair and eyes could be both caring and fierce.

Laura had always had a soft spot for Jen too, and whenever Clare had popped in, she always gave the both of them drinks and food on the house.

If not because she was fond of them, then at least because without young Jen, Laura knew that

Albatross

Geoff wouldn't manage alone in the kitchen, regardless of how fast he could move.

Something that had always tickled Clare when she visited was Laura's jumpers. Every day she wore an identical woollen jumper, be it green or yellow or blue or red, or any colour under the sun for that matter.

Clare had always been convinced that Laura had hundreds of these jumpers all lined up in her wardrobe, all in varying shades of every colour and design, and found the whole idea quite ridiculous and hilarious.

Eventually, late into the night, the last of the guests, and more often than not the rowdiest of the lot, were shooed out of the door by Laura, though admittedly quite some time past closing.

Jen was just about finished cleaning up in the kitchen, scrubbing and drying the metal work surfaces ready for the next day.

Soon enough she bid Geoff and Laura and the waiters and waitresses, whose names she could not recall, goodnight, informing them that she was off to meet Clare so that they could walk home together.

"Ok dear…" Laura replied, smiling warmly, though the look in her eyes was not dissimilar to the look in Geoff's.

"Stay safe…" The portly chef called after Jen as she disappeared into the night, and once she had vanished his gaze met Laura's, and they both took a deep, shuddering breath.

Geoff tentatively, almost even nervously, led Laura into the kitchen and reached out with one enormously pudgy hand to the fridge beside where Jen had been working.

Opening the door slowly, allowing the cold air to rush out with a slight hiss, they both peered inside.

The sight that greeted them came as no surprise really, but they both sighed audibly still.

On the top shelf sat a lovely looking sweet, on a plate decorated with drizzles of sauce: a piece of strawberry cheesecake that had been one of the dessert specials that evening.

Beneath it lay a piece of paper with a note scrawled across it.

Clare xxx

Jen always, every night and day that she worked, left a sweet in the fridge for her sister, and had done ever since she'd started at The Rusty Oak.

She didn't anymore, but there had once been a time when, instead of Jen having to go and meet her, Clare would come to find her sister before Jen finished work. She would sit and eat the sweet Jen always left for her, or even sometimes, if the weather permitted in the afternoons and evenings, Clare would come and sit out in the garden upon the decking.

Nowadays though, Jen always finished before Clare arrived, and she never came in the afternoons or evenings anymore.

Still though, always hopeful, Jen never failed to prepare a sweet for her sister, and Laura sighed again, this time somehow even more sadly.

Albatross

Her gaze dropped as she scraped Clare's sweet into the bin, and washed up the empty plate, knowing that if she didn't, it would only sit there.

She wished it wasn't the case, but sadly, Jen's sister never visited her at The Rusty Oak anymore.

That didn't stop Jen from wanting however, clinging to the blind hope that one day Clare would return.

Skylight Nights on Sea View Side

The front door to Keepers Cottage swung open and flooded the street with yellow light for a moment. Soon enough though Dyra heard footsteps in the hallway and the door clicked shut again.

"You're back early…" Dyra commented, drying her hands and glancing at her watch as she stepped round from the kitchen.

"Yeah." Jen replied simply, slinging her bag from her shoulder and unzipping her hoody. Her cheeks were flushed and she was breathing quite heavily. "We got home quicker than usual…"

"I see…" Her mother replied, though her brow furrowed with concern. "Is everything ok?"

"Yeah, fine thanks." Jen replied, heading immediately for the stairs. "Clare and I are going up for a bit…"

"Okay…" Dyra replied cautiously. "Let me know if you need anything…"

"We will…" Jen called back behind her, but she had already rounded the corner at the top of the landing and was out of sight.

"Mom really does worry when you shut off like that, you know…" Clare commented, her tone verging on reproachful as Jen climbed the second flight of stairs and opened the painted white door to her bedroom.

"I don't mean to…" Jen replied, her tone low and guilt-ridden.

"She just wants to know you're ok…" Clare pressed, pushing uncomfortable buttons that only she knew of.

"Yes…" Jen sighed, her tone exasperated. "I know…"

But Clare had made her point, and there was no need for her to make Jen feel worse. She just watched as her sister pulled off her clothes from work and rummaged around through her wooden chest of drawers for a clean set.

Jen found yet another hoody and a pair of jeans, and turned to pull them on, catching a glimpse of herself in the mirror as she did so.

She was thin, scrawny even, for she had lost a lot of weight recently. It hadn't been her intention; she'd just had no appetite of late. Her body looked weak and malnourished, and her arms and legs were stick thin.

Looking away, ignoring what she saw, Jen pulled her jeans on vigorously, faded blue and frayed here and there, and then chucked her hoody on just by itself.

Clare looked around her sister's room, biting her lip slightly as she surveyed the unkempt result of months of her younger sister's decline.

Jen's room was the highest in the house and at the front, on road view side, directly above the front door. The walls were white like the door and plain, with no pictures or posters. Only the mirror hung over to the left, beside the chest of drawers. The ceiling was slanted, as they were directly beneath the roof.

One window was set over the other side of the room in the ceiling, and another was on the front wall overlooking the front garden and the road.

A dusty TV that hadn't been used for months stood abandoned on her sister's bedside table, next to the single bed covered by a ruffled blue quilt that was hardly ever slept in, and a half empty bookcase sat lonesome and forgotten against the only remaining wall.

As Clare surveyed, Jen began to rummage once again, only this time not for clothes. Within moments she laid hands upon what she was after, and pulled a small Walkman CD player, old and outdated and battered, from beneath a pile of clothes.

Clare couldn't help but smile.

She had bought Jen that CD player years ago for Christmas one winter, and she had treasured it ever since. It was old and tatty and used almost beyond belief, but to her sister Clare knew it was priceless.

Jen then pulled an A4 sized black felt case from beneath her bed, and turned back to her older sister.

"Ready Clare?" She asked expectantly, all traces of remorse gone.

"Always." Clare replied with a gentle smile. "Lead the way."

Jen tucked the black case under her arm and stuffed her Walkman and a pair of earphones into her pocket.

Sidling over to the window set in the ceiling, moving with sudden eagerness round her bed, Jen pulled up the handle and pushed the window as high

Albatross

as it would go. It took her a few attempts, and she struggled perhaps more than she should have done, but eventually the window made it high enough and for her to hear the audible click of it locking in place.

Delving into her pocket and pulling out her Walkman, Jen reached out of the window and lodged it carefully behind a tile on the slanted roof, as she did almost every night, so that it didn't slide down and off the edge.

It had taken her a few goes to get the knack of this, and a few times she had very nearly lost it altogether.

She placed the black case beside it, lodging that too behind a tile, and then rested one hand either side of the windowsill. Jumping as high as she could, and hauling with all her might, though again this took a fair few goes, Jen heaved herself up and out, over the edge of the windowsill, and onto the slate roof.

Though she'd lost weight, this hadn't got any easier, for without food she was weak and fragile, and had no strength whatsoever.

Nonetheless, she thought little of it, instead grabbing her case and CD player and standing up to look upon the night.

Since her bedroom was front facing, she emerged onto road view side, and looked down at the dark lane seemingly so far below her.

A lazy, cold breeze wound its way between Jen's legs and through her hoody, forcing her to shiver and draw a sharp breath.

She turned carefully and ascended up to the apex of the roof, climbing over and moving steadily onto the opposite face.

Sea view side.

And indeed, as always, in the distance even through the dim night, she could just about make out the breaking of the waves on the shoreline, off towards the horizon.

Squatting down and perching for a moment on the slanted tiles, Jen found the same comfortable spot that she had last night, and the night before, and the one before that, and indeed almost every night before that too.

Though the wind was not all that strong, she clutched her Walkman and the felt case tightly, as if they might be ripped from her grasp at any moment.

Tucking her Walkman safely into her lap, Jen unzipped the black case round three sides and opened it to reveal several dozen CD wallets, some full to the brim, and others empty and unused.

She began to slowly flick through the CD's, just about able to make out the writing on them in the dark. Many of them were just blank discs that she and Clare had burned songs on to, and then in their haste scribbled a seemingly appropriate name on the front in black marker.

Some were very worn and scratched and clearly well used, while others hadn't been touched for some time; as seemed to be the case with many of Jen's belongings nowadays.

She paused for a moment.

Summer 12

Albatross

That was a while ago now, she thought to herself.

She remembered making that one with Clare after they'd spent the week away with friends. Though, now she recalled one of the best weeks of her life, the memory seemed so long lost and faded, as if almost it didn't even belong to her: as if it had happened in another lifetime altogether.

Gym Songs

Now that one was a little more recent, but not much, if she was honest with herself.

Although, she was never honest with herself anymore.

"Jennifer! Dinner!" She heard her mom's voice call faintly from far below.

She sidled over to the open skylight, just nipping back over the top of the roof, and silently pushed it to. She didn't close it entirely, but just enough to make it look like she and Clare had gone back out, when their mother inevitably came looking for them.

Besides, she wasn't hungry.

She just wanted to be left alone.

But then, as she sat back down and flicked her CD case over again, the next disc had writing scrawled across it that left a pit in Jen's stomach.

From Clare xx

"You haven't listened to that one for ages…" Clare commented dryly, speaking for the first time since they'd climbed out onto the rooftop.

She sat directly beside her younger sister in just a T-shirt and a thin pair of black joggers, though she seemed not in the least bit bothered by the cold, and peered over Jen's shoulder at the wallets of CD's on her lap.

"I know…" Jen replied, sighing, her voice sobered considerably. "It used to be my favourite…"

"Why don't you give it a go?" Clare suggested, her tone encouraging.

"No…" Jen replied quietly, her voice dropping to a whisper. "I can't…" Though her words said one thing, clearly she wasn't sure, and her eyes darted to her sister's beautiful, stricken face.

"Why not?" Clare asked, her voice wavering, clearly hurt.

"I…I can't…" Was all Jen managed, only able to repeat what she'd already said.

She quickly flicked over to the next wallet of discs, not even looking to see what it was, pulled it out, and immediately shoved it into her Walkman. She rammed her earphones into her ears and hit play, greeted in an instant by drowning drumbeats and lyrics that she knew all too well, but could not recall.

Clare said not another word, knowing when she wasn't wanted.

She simply sat on the rooftop, huddled close beside her troubled sister, though, as much as she desperately wanted to, she didn't put her arm around Jen.

It had been dark before, but after not too long it was nearly pitch black, for the stars and the moon were shrouded by the clouds; they were haunting ghosts floating above endlessly, pushed this way and that by the careless winds.

A cruel chill crept viciously over Jen's skin and bit at her exposed face terribly.

The clouds above had initially trapped some of the heat of the day, but in the occasionally lashing winds they parted obediently here and there.

That was a mixed blessing however, for even though they allowed the odd slither of light through, at the same time they let all of that encased heat escape up and out into the vast universe, racing out towards the ocean of stars that swam endlessly around the crescent moon.

For a second even the kind moon bathed Jen in its glowing light as she sat atop the roof gazing out at the shimmering ocean, no longer grey or black, but glistening white in the rich moonlight.

However, even as she looked out over the gorgeous view laid down before her, Jen still sat shoulder deep in gloomy thought, wrapped in melancholy so bottomless that it clutched her awfully tightly to its breast.

She glanced across at her sister sat beside her for a moment, and Clare positively glowed in the moonlight, her face radiant and her eyes untouched.

She had always been the prettier of the two of them, and now, at the very least in Jen's eyes, that was truer than ever.

"Jenny…" Clare breathed then, breaking the doomed silence that had fallen over them.

The clouds sealed together again and cast the two sisters into darkness once more.

"Is it going to be like this forever…?" She asked her younger sister, tears welling in her perfect eyes.

Somehow Jen heard Clare's words perfectly, even over the sound of the music buried in her ears.

She sighed and pulled her earphones out, knowing she could not escape this.

Someone else looking in might not have known exactly what Clare meant by that, but Jen knew different.

She knew exactly what her sister meant.

Put simply, Clare was asking Jen if she would be miserable for the rest of her life.

But whether Jen wanted to admit that or not, was an entirely different matter.

She took a very deep breath, biting the bullet, but not knowing where this would lead.

"I can't see the end…" She eventually replied, and that was perhaps the most honest statement she had uttered for months.

Clare was the only person she didn't have to hide from.

She couldn't even if she tried.

Her sister saw right into her very heart.

It was so hard to be as honest with other people as she was with Clare.

"That makes me sad, Jenny…" Clare replied honestly.

Jen sighed, but didn't speak. She only turned up the music on her Walkman and put her earphones back in, desperate to drown out the truth.

"You really ought to tell mom, you know…" Clare said then, her voice carrying a reproachful tone once again, and Jen glanced nervously over to her at her words.

"No…" Her younger sister replied quickly. "I can't…"

"You promised her." Clare pointed out, and quite rightly so. "You promised you'd tell Mandy too. You can't keep lying to them…"

"Please don't tell them!" Jen almost begged her sister then, her voice pleading and desperate and stricken.

Clare pursed her lips and exhaled deeply, her glistening eyes sorrowful.

"You know I can't tell them…"

And on those final, grief-stricken words, Jen did not reply, and turned instead back to her distraught gazing.

Clare joined her, sitting with her as she always did. But no matter how long the night wore on, nor how deeply the cold sunk into Jen's very bones, still Clare did not put her arm round her sister to warm her.

It wouldn't have made any difference.

She Who Interferes

"How did you sleep sweetheart?" Dyra asked her youngest daughter the following morning, an hour or so after sunrise had broken on the misty horizon over to the East.

In truth, Jen was groggy and stiff and sore, to say the very least. She had at some point crawled back inside her window during the night, but most definitely not before the cold had ruined her joints, and now her whole body ached.

"Yeah, fine." She lied, naturally.

Taking a single bite of toast Jen stood up to take her plate to the sink, whilst her mother still hovered cautiously over her own unfinished breakfast.

"I thought you'd gone out again…" Dyra continued. "I came up to get you to tell you dinner was ready, but I couldn't find you…"

"No…" Jen uttered, pausing at first as if there wasn't anything else to follow. Eventually though, cautiously, she continued. "We were up on the roof…"

"Oh…I see…" Her mother concluded, her tone clearly disapproving. "You know I don't like that, Jennifer…" She continued, her words cautionary. "It's dangerous…"

Jen only sighed.

Yes, she knew her mother didn't like it.

Albatross

But, at the same time, her mother knew that she knew. And, in turn, Dyra also knew that she'd been going out onto the roof for months now.

Just, complicated as it was, neither of them wanted to argue the point.

Dyra let it drop, and instead drew a deep breath to introduce the tender subject that had been her original intention in the first place.

"Caroline's coming over today…" She breached as gently as she could, though, it's near impossible to be subtle when you're using a battering ram.

Jen's initial response was a look shot across the kitchen that mixed perfectly seriousness, disgust and despair all into one.

"Now…" Dyra attempted to salvage the situation before it got out of hand. "Please try to be polite…"

"Where's she been now then!?" Jen suddenly exploded, all of her anger multiplying and escalating, completely out of control in an instant. "What's she coming to show off this time!?"

"Please…" Her mother attempted, but her efforts were futile.

"She's just coming to tell me how to live my life again!!" Jen blurted, tears streaming down her face all of a sudden.

"Jen!!" Dyra cried desperately.

But it was too late.

The damage was already done.

"NO!!" Jen yelled in a note of sheer finality. She fled the kitchen immediately, racing upstairs shaking uncontrollably.

Two flights of stairs later she huddled on the floor leaning against the chest of drawers in her bedroom, sobbing and gasping, though she wasn't entirely sure why. It took quite some time for Jen to regain some semblance of composure, but luckily Dyra left her to it.

Having heard the commotion, Clare sat by Jen's side the whole time, silent and unmoving.

Her mere presence was comforting, as Jen slowly managed to calm herself.

She had never really been all that emotional, and rarely succumbed to her feelings in such a dramatic way. But of late, for some reason, she had found it more and more difficult to contain her rushing and raging emotions.

Depression and anger and various other uncontrollable and immature feelings gripped her all too often nowadays, throwing her into a deep pit of suffering that, no matter how hard she tried, she simply could not climb out of.

Now, saying that, Caroline was not the most likeable of characters.

She was Dyra's big sister, and in turn, made anything that was her baby sister's business her own. That, unfortunately, included the ways in which Dyra raised her children, and she more often than not looked down her nose at them in the most obnoxious manner possible.

Revelling in her own success, if you could call it that, she was, in a phrase, a stuck up cow.

Married three times and then in turn divorced three times, the main quality that she sought in men was money. Consequently, out of her three marriages, she had made herself a small fortune, claiming all sorts of absurdities that quite simply weren't true.

She had two children of her own, neither of whom she ever made any attempt to see, and she only ever came to visit her baby sister Dyra to gloat about her latest holiday, and to see if Jen had sorted her life out yet.

Cruel as that all might sound, that was, in a nutshell, Caroline.

However, it made no odds.

She was on her way, and that was that.

It was several hours later, once Jen had had ample time to gather her emotions, and to allow for the joy of it all to sink in, that Caroline eventually pulled up outside Keepers Cottage.

Of course, as was relatively standard, she was driving a brand new BMW: a shiny new blue with all the bells and whistles.

Jen twitched with barely concealed frustration.

Despite her mother's best efforts, Jen wore a plain T-shirt over her scrawny frame, and loose fitting jeans.

"Try to relax, Jenny." Clare advised quietly as the click clack of Caroline's heels up the pathway to their door announced her imminent arrival. "And try not to slap her…" She added, grinning eagerly.

"Thanks…" Jen whispered back dryly.

Clare was wearing a light blue dress with floral orange patterns splashed across it.

As always, she looked lovely.

Suddenly their front door burst open and Caroline swept inside with arms flailing and tones wailing.

Jen couldn't help but hold back a snigger as her aunt appeared. She always wore a big fur coat, regardless of the weather, heels of at least six inches, and bangles all up her wrists.

The sight always for some reason made Jen think of Cruella de Vil, and Clare too concealed a smirk, knowing exactly what her younger sister was thinking.

"My darling baby sister!" Caroline exclaimed dramatically, exaggerating her entrance as theatrically as humanly possible, and extending her arms immediately out to Dyra.

Shopping bags hung off her wrists, as they always did, and her bangles clattered and jangled obnoxiously.

"Hello Caroline." Jen's mother replied stiffly, embracing her sister reluctantly. Her big sister would have none of it however, and flung her arms about Dyra and gasped melodramatically.

"Oh! It's been far too long!" She cried.

Jen winced and cringed visibly, and Clare stifled another snigger.

Caroline turned to Jen and her eyes seemed to narrow warily and suspiciously, though the action seemed subconscious.

There was no over the top greeting to follow; she simply looked Dyra's youngest daughter up and down in what appeared to be the most critical and judgemental manner possible.

"You've lost a lot of weight, Jennifer." Were the first words to pass Caroline's lips, rolling off her tongue with easy distaste and disapproval. "You look like you need a good meal."

Jen had expected nothing less and, much to Caroline's displeasure, didn't bite.

"Hello Caroline." She replied, though her voice simply dripped with undisguised loathing.

"Aren't you feeding her, Dyra?" Caroline questioned her baby sister then, glancing back around.

"Erm…Jen…" Dyra started, not knowing quite what to say. "Jen's fine…" She concluded lamely, and Caroline just sniffed in response and pulled two of the shopping bags hung on her arm into one hand, and held them out to her ungrateful niece.

"I've brought you gifts." She announced, very formally, dropping the bags unceremoniously at Jen's feet.

Her long, false nails caught on the string at the last moment and the bags toppled to one side on the floor, with what sounded like a distinct crack.

"Why, thank you." Jen replied coldly, making no attempt to pick them up.

Caroline flicked her long, dyed blonde hair out of her face, revealing the full extent of her awful fake eyelashes and tan, which seemed to radiate a sickly orange rather than brown.

Very classy.

Jen's expression, however, was growing darker by the moment, and her mother sensed the danger as it encroached.

"Why don't we…" Dyra attempted to intervene, hoping to cut off the arrivals before bloodshed ensued.

Unfortunately, she failed.

"Have you brought anything for Clare, Caroline?" Jen asked then, her voice piercing the air like a knife coated in poisonous venom.

Her aunt looked down at her quite seriously then, puffing up her own self-importance, and replied in a tone that made Jen's blood boil and seethe.

"No, Jen, don't be absurd. Of course I haven't." She replied bluntly, sneering as she spoke.

That was it.

Caroline had been there all of about two minutes, and already Jen was ready to explode.

She felt her rage building inside of her, and it swelled and rose and multiplied so fast and in such a charging rush that she felt as if she was going to burst: her emotions completely out of control.

"Don't do it Jenny…" Clare warned then, sighing regretfully and looking between her younger sister and their horrible aunt.

Jen paused, stuck between a rock and a hard place.

Silence hung for a moment before Clare spoke again.

"She isn't worth it…"

Jen's dreadful, uncontrollable wrath caught on the tip of her tongue, concealed within a single breath, and with seemingly inhuman self-control, at her sister's will, she swallowed it down, burying it deep inside.

Without another word Jen turned for the front door and departed.

"And where do you think…" Caroline began, but Jen didn't hear her finish, for she slammed the door tremendously behind her and headed immediately down the garden and out onto the road, turning instinctively towards the beach.

"Jen?" A voice suddenly called, startling her in her rage.

Jen looked up and, completely out of the blue, Mandy appeared, catching her totally off guard.

"Oh, erm…I…Mandy…" Was all she managed, tripping over herself repeatedly, and her quickly dissipating fury was thrown completely.

Jen's emotions were up and down like a rollercoaster.

"Is everything alright?" Mandy asked. Concern was evident in her soft voice, always so gentle and thoughtful.

Her sleek, black hair was tied back in a neat ponytail and her brown eyes were somehow all seeing, as if every time Jen looked into them they gazed right into her very soul.

She liked Mandy, but that was one of the reasons Jen always dreaded her visits.

One of them.

"Erm, yes…I'm fine, thank you…" Jen managed to reply, still stumbling over her tongue and shaking slightly.

Mandy was not convinced.

"What's happened?" She asked immediately, glancing over her glasses that were perched delicately on her nose, looking briefly between Jen and the front door to Keepers Cottage.

Mandy had quite a pale complexion, but not so that she looked ill. The aura that she held was most definitely one of professionalism and assertiveness, tinged with a generous helping of care and understanding: a rather unusual mix of qualities that most certainly made her stand out, and in fact made her absurdly attractive.

She wore black trousers, smart dress shoes and a white blouse, partly covered by a cardigan that stretched halfway down her arms and pulled in at her petite waist. Clutched at her generous breast, between folded arms, she held her black portfolio case that she always carried with her when making her visits.

"Oh, nothing…" Jen lied, though very badly this time, and Mandy looked at her reproachfully.

"Jen…" She said calmly then, tilting her head forward slightly, raising her eyebrows and pursing her lips thoughtfully.

Jen sighed.

Of course, it was no use lying to her.

"Caroline's here…" She admitted, as if that explained everything.

"Ah…" Mandy replied, suddenly understanding, for indeed that scrap of knowledge did in fact explain an awful lot.

Jen sighed, and Mandy looked at the poor girl, only six years or so younger than herself, in a way that spoke volumes of compassion for what she had been through, and in fact was still going through.

"Your mom phoned me yesterday to say you had to work…" She noted then, changing the subject as smoothly as she could. "But I was coming past today anyway, and so I thought I'd pop by to see how you are…"

"Thank you." Jen replied automatically. "Yeah, sorry, I had to work."

"Don't be silly! Don't apologise!" Mandy laughed then. "Are you still enjoying things at The Rusty Oak?"

"Yeah…" Jen replied elusively, glancing down at the ground.

Mandy's expression hardened slightly.

"How have things been?" She asked, her voice quite a lot more serious. "Any repeat occurrences? Any new episodes?"

"No, no…" Jen replied as reassuringly as she could manage, though, admittedly, her words were not all that convincing. "Everything's fine…" She concluded rather lamely.

"I see…" Mandy commented, clear in her tone exactly how believable Jen had been.

Jen spied movement from the house then through one of the downstairs windows, and shifted uncomfortably as she caught Caroline's gaze for a moment, watching the two of them talking outside.

Of course, Mandy noticed this too, and kindly released Jen from her suffering.

"I won't keep you then…" She said smiling, and Jen looked at her gratefully.

Though sometimes it didn't seem like it, when she made her visits, Mandy was most definitely on Jen's side, and came as close to understanding her as anybody probably could, excluding Clare, naturally.

"Thank you." Jen replied, relief coursing through her veins.

"But I will be coming to visit again, soon. Very soon." Mandy assured her, clearly not happy with what she'd seen already that day.

Jen winced inwardly, but nodded and smiled in response.

"Okay…" She said, turning to continue off towards the beach. "Thank you…"

Soon, though never soon enough, the beach was in sight, and Jen's pace quickened more and more with every step she took.

She just wanted to be alone.

She needed to be alone.

And so, naturally, whenever she felt like that, she knew what would come next, without a shadow of a doubt.

"Jenny!" A familiar voice called on the wind, and even lost in thought as deeply as she might have been, she knew exactly who it was.

There was only one person in the world who had ever called her that.

Sure enough, as she halted her frantic pace and stopped and turned to look, the wind lashing harsh and cold against her face, there was Clare.

She still wore the light blue dress with the orange floral patterns on it, and the material that came down to about her knees whipped wildly about her well defined legs. The rest of the dress pulled tightly to her slender, yet perfectly filled frame, accentuating her body in all the right places.

She had been too angry to notice it before, but now, as ever, Jen stood in absolute awe of her sister's beauty.

Clare didn't even have a coat or a jumper with her, but it didn't matter. Like always, the cold never bothered her.

She didn't even feel it.

Fortunately, even in her vast fury, Jen had had the foresight to grab a jacket as she'd stormed out of the house, and pulled it more tightly around her scrawny frame.

She always felt the cold. Especially now she'd lost so much weight.

Jen smiled, though admittedly a little half-heartedly, as her older sister approached.

"You're always running off at the moment!" Clare laughed as she slowed, smiling, her voice bubbly and unaffected by the morning's debacle.

"Sorry…" Jen replied, though her response was half-hearted too.

"Where are you going?" Clare asked then, even though she already knew the answer.

"I'm heading down to the beach…" Jen replied automatically.

"Of course!" Clare laughed again. "Where else would you be headed!?"

Jen sighed but didn't reply, and simply turned and continued towards the coast, trudging now towards the rocks where she would sit and wallow, and hopefully drown, in her own misery.

Clare frowned, frustrated, but followed in tow, and didn't say another word.

Jen pulled her jacket ever more tightly about her neck as the wind cut horribly through her body, and the brine on the air bit and lashed at her face.

Her sister remained indifferent to the cold.

"Jen!" Another voice called then, though the sound of it was partly lost to the wind.

Who could this possibly be now? She thought to herself as she looked over her shoulder and down the coastal path that stretched along the beach, parallel to the sand and rocks upon which she was about to step.

But when she laid eyes upon whom the voice belonged to, a lump caught in her throat.

The figure approached and he smiled reassuringly.

"Jen!" The police officer exclaimed. "How are you?" He asked. "I haven't seen you for months!"

"Officer Mahoney…" She greeted him, whom she knew very well, and perhaps not for the right reasons. "I'm okay, thanks…" She lied. "How are you?"

Police officer Jim Mahoney was a good man.

He was handsome, with blonde hair, blue eyes, and a bushy moustache that very nearly protruded over his top lip.

A thick set chap, though at the same time very tall, Jen had always imagined he could be very intimidating when he needed to be.

"Oh, you know…" He replied with a slight chuckle. "Keeping busy."

Jen didn't know, but she smiled and nodded anyway.

He was always nice to her, and had tried to help her when she'd needed it the most.

He was very perceptive, but in very different ways to Mandy, and so couldn't always pinpoint exactly what Jen needed in the way she could.

"What have you been up to?" He asked then, clearly oblivious to the subtle clues that Mandy had so easily picked up on.

"I'm still at The Rusty Oak." Jen replied, shifting her weight from one foot to the other.

"Oh! Great!" He replied enthusiastically, though he glanced at his watch as he spoke. "Anyway, I won't keep you, and I've got to get back. I just wanted to say hello! Glad you're okay!"

"Well, thank you…" Jen replied, though her words were continually swept away by the heavy wind.

"Have a good day! Stay safe!" He offered then, and turned immediately to leave, disappearing round the corner and out of sight.

For a moment, after that brief whirlwind of a conversation, there was blissful silence, before Clare's voice broke it seemingly louder than the screeching gale, even though she spoke in the quietest of tones.

"Well…" She commented, emphasising her words. "Aren't we the popular one today…"

Jen pulled a face at her older sister.

"I just want to be left alone…" She grumbled.

"I'll leave if I'm not wanted…" Clare replied with a withering look, perhaps more harshly than she'd intended.

Jen shot her a desperate, pleading glance in return.

"You know that's not what I meant…" She countered, and Clare nodded in rueful agreement.

"They just don't understand, Jenny…" Clare tried to comfort her little sister.

"Nobody understands…" Jen replied glumly.

"Do you?" Clare asked her then, turning to face her quite purposefully, forcing Jenny to look her right in the eyes.

Jen sighed and breathed the truth that her older sister already knew.

"I don't want to…"

"You really have got to stop this!" Caroline argued, her tone urging and forceful. She waved her arms madly as she spoke, towering over her baby sister, her bangles jangling as she went on.

"You don't know how hard it is!" Dyra opposed, attempting almost in vain to defy her sister's rule.

And so she should have done.

Caroline had no grounds whatsoever, besides the fact that she was a bully.

"Oh boo hoo!" Her big sister exclaimed then, once again throwing her arms up in a grand, theatrical gesture. "So shit happens! Get over it! This is getting bloody ridiculous now! It's time to move on!"

"Caroline…" Dyra attempted again.

But it was of little use.

She was off on one.

"Find yourself another man!" She declared then. "That's what you need! And you need to sort that little brat out…"

"ENOUGH! CAROLINE!" Dyra suddenly boomed, snapping and exploding at her sister from completely out of the blue. "LEAVE JEN ALONE!!"

Taken aback for a moment, stunned by her baby sister's sudden outburst, Caroline found no words.

"Stop coming over here and bullying her!!" Dyra continued. "She's having a hard enough time as it is!!"

"I'm not bullying her…" Caroline argued, but Dyra had heard enough.

"When she gets back, I want you gone!" She seethed.

"And so where's she gone!?" Caroline countered, recovering swiftly, reassuming her lofty, self-importance. "To the beach!?" Her tone disapproving and distasteful.

"I imagine so…" Dyra breathed dangerously.

"That's all she does!" Caroline exclaimed. "Doesn't she do anything else!? All she did the last time I was here was go and sit on those bloody rocks! Doesn't she have any friends!? Or a job!?"

"She still works at The Rusty Oak!" Dyra argued defensively, though she shouldn't have allowed Caroline the pleasure.

"She needs to grow up and get a life!" Caroline stated in a very matter of fact way.

"What!? Like you!?" Dyra spat back then, her words laced with poison. "Fleecing the richest bloke she can find and then moving on to the next!? How many have you got on the go at the moment!? Three!? Four!?"

"Oh bollocks to you both!!" Caroline erupted. "So I suppose she's just gonna sit on that beach for the rest of her life!? She'll eventually just rot away and die there she's lost that much weight! But no one will bloody notice!!"

"LEAVE HER ALONE!!" Dyra screamed, her voice reaching a towering crescendo that shook the glasses and crockery in the kitchen cabinets.

"WHO'S GONNA KNOW!?" Caroline shrieked back. "Is she out there on her own!? Just for a change!?"

Without a second thought Dyra responded, full of anger, not even thinking about what she was saying.

"SHE'S WITH CLARE!! NOW BACK OFF!!"

Caroline gave her furious baby sister a withering look, but said no more.

Within seconds, with nothing more to say, she had composed herself, gathered her things, and left.

She abandoned her baby sister, leaving her standing alone in the kitchen, silently shaking and seething, her fists clenched so tightly that her knuckles were white.

The sound of her big sister's car starting outside barely even registered in Dyra's mind, and it was only as the sound of the engine faded away into the distance that Dyra's legs gave way beneath her, and she collapsed back against the kitchen wall.

She slid down to the floor in a crumpled heap, heaving and sobbing, having finally realised exactly

what she'd said, and tears of both grief and
desperation streaked openly down her cheeks.

Deacon

By the time Jen returned from the beach Caroline was long gone, but the atmosphere still remained, lingering like a bad smell.

She swept in through the front door, opening it silently and retrieving her rucksack in what could have been mistaken for a single movement.

Dyra heard the brief scuffle of footsteps and looked round from the kitchen, but saw only her youngest daughter's back as she closed the door again behind her, making for The Rusty Oak.

Jen wound her way through the lanes once more, only this time she took absolutely no notice of the cold or the cars or the cottages.

By the time she was halfway there she was completely in a world of her own, numb to everything around her, and even when the odd car did drive past she barely even noticed.

No horns were honked, and so she could only presume that not even Geoff passed her, but then, at the same time, there was no way she could have been sure.

Clouds swarmed above like vultures circling their prey, honing in on their target coldheartedly, yet also in a way that was only the most natural of worldly events.

It was just before The Rusty Oak came into sight when the heavens eventually decided to open, dumping everything they had rather unceremoniously upon Jen, swamping her completely.

She ran the last leg of her journey, holding her bag above her head in a futile attempt to remain dry.

Unsurprisingly, when she arrived, she looked like an underfed, drowned rat.

Stumbling into the kitchen, making her way this time round to the back door, the sight of Geoff greeted her, humming quietly to himself as he marinated chicken, stirred bubbling stew, sliced vegetables, and put the finishing touches to a banana split, somehow all at once.

"Good day!" He greeted Jen enthusiastically as she entered, smiling broadly at her.

"Hello Geoff." Jen replied mildly, her thoughts distracted as she scooped her dripping hair up into a ponytail, ringing the worst of the water out of it as she did so, and pulled an apron about her to cover her wet clothes.

Immediately Jen set to work, having no real reason to dawdle, and she silently prepared for the rush that they both knew would shortly come. Geoff hummed and occasionally whistled, whilst Jen worked in comparative quiet, neither speaking nor humming.

The smells of the kitchen wafted out as waiters and waitresses drifted to and fro, carrying hints of beef and lamb and pork with them as they went.

Regularly Jen wiped the metal work surfaces down, cleaned plates and chopping boards and cutlery, stocked and restocked the fridge, and filled and boiled the kettle, and refilled and boiled it again, over and over.

Soon enough, working fluidly together, yet also, Geoff thought, with slight apprehension in the air, the two of them delved into the sudden rush of orders that came flurrying through to them. Between tasks he frequently glanced over to Jen, admittedly a little concerned.

After a couple of hours they were graced with a slight lull in demand, and Jen automatically set about fixing Clare's sweet.

Today it was chocolate cake, and Jen cut a generous slice for her older sister and decorated it with drizzles of sauce and various other vibrant dressings.

Within minutes it found its way into the fridge, with the customary note of course, and Jen attended to the starter orders that had just come in.

Geoff looked over again as she worked, and this time his gaze lingered for rather a lot longer as he watched her write the note. His eyes looked troubled and he pulled a slight grimace of a face.

"Are you meeting Clare after work?" He asked Jen then, simply unable to stand the silence any longer.

"Yes…" Jen only replied at first, stuffing some mushrooms. "We're walking home together…"

"Ah…I see…" Geoff replied. "How is she?" He asked then.

"She's fine, thank you." Jen responded, her tone level, still concentrating on her mushrooms. Though, Geoff got the distinct impression that the mushrooms weren't entirely the reason she was avoiding giving him much more than those simple, unenlightening answers to his questions.

He drew breath again, preparing to take the plunge: something he would never usually have done, but things were just getting far too out of hand. However, right at that moment, Laura came racing in, wearing a green jumper today, and waving a handful of order tickets in the air.

"Party of fifteen!" She exclaimed, smiling joyously, for how she loved to work. "Mains to follow!" And she pinned the tickets to the board and swept out of the kitchen again like a hurricane, leaving destruction in her wake.

Geoff sighed.

The moment was lost.

He wouldn't question Jen now.

And so began the waltz.

Day wore into dusk, and dusk laboured into night, and Geoff and Jen pushed on.

Eventually the night drew to a close and Jen finished up the last of her jobs before leaving to meet her sister. She hung her apron and grabbed her bag, bid goodbye briefly to Geoff and Laura, and headed immediately for the door, pulling her hair from its ponytail with great relief, and running her hands quickly through it.

It was still damp, but she wasn't really all that bothered.

They both watched her go with worry in their eyes, for, as always nowadays, she seemed so disheartened.

However, as she opened the heavy wooden door to leave, not really concentrating on what she was doing, Jen didn't see the distorted figure approaching through the glass on the other side. Just as she looped her bag onto her shoulder, pulling the door open with her free hand, she stepped out and ploughed directly into the man stood beneath the archway on the doorstep.

Her bag slipped from her arm and fell to the floor with a dull thud, and Jen almost went careering backwards, for she had been hastening with some speed, head down and in her own world.

A strong hand reached out and caught her by the arm, keeping her from falling and steadying her so she could regain her balance.

Without even looking up, Jen stooped immediately to retrieve her rucksack, but somehow, without her even realising, he already had it in his other hand.

Jen's eyes swept upwards then and she felt as if they were opened for the first time in a very long time. Her gaze met his bluey green eyes and she was instantly fixated, and he seemed to see everything through those mysterious pools of undefined colour.

He was tall, quite a bit taller than her, and his sandy blonde hair looked ruffled, but strangely not in the least bit unkempt.

In the hazy light he looked to be in his early twenties. His face was well defined with high cheekbones, but did not appear too rugged, though there was an air about him that Jen felt most prominently, and which spoke volumes of much more life experience than merely twenty years.

"I…I'm sorry…" Jen mumbled, looking for words to fill the silence, for she could not tear her eyes away from his, though he seemed to stare back into hers quite calmly, holding her gaze eagerly.

Albatross

Without a word at first, he held her rucksack out and she clutched it back gratefully, though his free hand still lingered on her arm, and for some reason she didn't want him to remove it.

"Not at all…" He replied first, his voice pitched so that it sounded soft and worn all at once. "It was my fault. Are you okay?"

His question, at face value, might have been answered with a simple, 'yes, thank you, I'm fine'.

But, in reality, somehow, Jen could sense that wasn't the question he was really asking her.

She thought she was going crazy, and had absolutely no idea how to reply.

What he was asking her was very personal, and so deeply ingrained and relevant to all that she was faced with in her life, that his bluey green eyes seemed to pool with boundless concern and affection for her.

Within moments, Jen found herself embarrassed, and felt her cheeks flush furiously as she blushed bright red.

Instinctively, flight kicking in, she turned to leave, taking a rushed, though admittedly at the same time hesitant step out into the night.

But she didn't make it far, for he caught her now by the hand, not firmly, but just enough to stop her, and seemingly without a thought she spun to face him once again, powerless at his touch.

His eyes saw everything as they bore tenderly into her.

It was as if they looked right into her very soul, and Jen couldn't help but be drawn further and further into them.

Still, even as they stared at each other yet again, neither of them spoke another word.

Finally he smiled, melting Jen almost completely.

Her knees began to shake.

She felt a sudden rush surge through her body and her heart fluttered, though she had no idea why.

She had never felt this way before.

"Didn't I see you at the beach the other day?" He asked her then, finally breaking the silence that enveloped them.

Taken aback completely, Jen fumbled for words.

She had no idea.

There had been other people at the beach, undoubtedly there always were, but she never saw them.

She was never looking.

She only ever saw Clare.

"I…I'm…I…" She stumbled, floundering in her own embarrassment.

Luckily though, he rescued her, and perhaps not for the first, nor the last.

"Were you with somebody?" The stranger asked her.

"C…Clare…" Jen eventually managed.

What was happening to her?

"A friend of yours?" He enquired, tilting his head slightly to one side and smiling.

"My sister…" She replied, at last managing to string two words together without stammering.

"I see…" He replied mysteriously. "And is it her you're in such a rush to meet?" He asked, flitting his eyes to their hands, still touching, somehow seeming to be posing his words as a statement of fact, rather than a query.

"We, she…I'm meeting her…" Jen managed, though admittedly with great difficulty, returning to her stumbling as his eyes swept briefly over her, taking in everything about her in a single glance, or so it seemed at least.

Even still, he hadn't released her hand, and his hold was gentle and firm all at once. His fingers were warm against her cold skin, and she liked it.

As he spoke again, he released her from his grasp and she felt suddenly bitterly lost, and fell immediately into her deep, unending emptiness once more. It swallowed her whole in all its enormity, and Jen felt as though the ground had been wrenched out from beneath her feet.

She had been rescued, even if for barely a few minutes, and now, once let go, she plummeted into despair yet again.

How could this happen?

She couldn't let him go…

"I'd better let you go so you can meet her then…" He replied, as if confirming her deepest, darkest fears, and he tilted his head slightly in saddened acknowledgement.

But, hard as she tried, and as desperately as she might have wanted to, Jen could not find the words to reply. The rushing emotions that barraged her so heavily robbed her of her breath.

She managed a nod, but no more, and only barely at that.

Turning to leave, distraught, his words like rough velvet stopped her once again.

"Can I ask your name?" He requested politely, raising his eyebrows almost unconsciously and turning his mouth up at the corners in a cheeky smile that, if she had not been so deeply off balance, would have told Jen volumes about this particular young man.

"Jen…" She eventually managed, her voice barely a whisper. "I'm Jen…"

He bowed his head slightly and opened his hand in a rather unseemly grand gesture to her: something that she wasn't expecting.

She felt the strange and burning urge to reach out and grab it.

She so desperately wanted to.

But she didn't.

"Until we meet again then, Jen…" The stranger bade her a gracious farewell.

And in that moment something overwhelmed young Jennifer that she had never before in her life experienced. Considering that she had barely felt anything besides misery and dejection for so long now, it sent her blood coursing and racing through her veins like wildfire, stirring her overwhelmed emotions into a maddened frenzy.

She wanted him to kiss her.

She wanted to lean in so that he could.

And somehow, she could see that he knew it too.

But he only smiled, seemingly ever the gentleman, and after a few moments, her heart in her mouth, Jen managed to sir herself into movement and passed through the heavy wooden doorway that he still held open, and out into the cold of the night.

Her heart fluttered continuously, and she didn't feel like she had butterflies in her stomach as much as they swarmed through her entire body, colonising in her chest it seemed.

"Oh, and, by the way..." He called calmly after her, and she turned to face him one last time.

Her cheeks flushed afresh and her heart still pounded furiously against her ribs, lust filled for the first time in her life.

"I'm Deacon..."

Memoria Lane

That night, for the first night in a long time, when she arrived home, Jen didn't immediately race out onto the roof. When she appeared in the kitchen, pulling her hoody off over her head, her mother was pleasantly surprised to see her, especially after the incident with Caroline.

"How was work, sweetheart?" Dyra asked her youngest daughter.

"Yeah…I, good. It was good thanks. How are you?"

Immediately Dyra could tell that something wasn't quite right.

What had happened?

Perhaps she'd come to tell her what she'd been waiting to hear for so long now, one way or another.

Hopefully.

She'd been waiting for months.

But when Jen came and sat down, perching across the table from her mother, there was something in her daughter's eyes that Dyra had never seen before. And she had absolutely no idea what it was.

Not that that was anything new.

"Are you okay?" Dyra asked.

"Yeah, I think so…" Her daughter replied.

"You think so?" Dyra questioned immediately, concerned, as a parent always will be. "Did you get home okay? What's happened!?"

Albatross

"No, nothing, it's fine. I got home fine." Jen reassured her, of course knowing exactly why she was asking that.

"So what is it?" Her mother pressed.

She thought she knew what her youngest daughter's next breath would be, but after a few more anxious moments, she realised in fact that she had been wrong. She was surprised. Pleasantly so, in fact, although she was still worried.

Taking a deep breath, Dyra decided it was time to take the plunge.

"Did you walk home with Clare?" She asked then, her tone cautious and her gaze upon her daughter warily.

"What? Oh, not in the end, no…." Came Jen's reply, which shocked her mother even more, so much so that Dyra could find no reply.

"Oh…" Was all she managed in her surprise.

"I think I might go to bed…" Jen stated then, rising slowly, and admittedly wearily to her feet.

"Okay, sweetheart…" Her mother replied, practically jumping to her feet also, not really knowing what to say or do.

"Goodnight. I'll see you in the morning." Jen said fondly then, bidding her mother a good night and embracing her before disappearing up the stairs, leaving Dyra sat alone and shocked in the kitchen.

Jen's sudden change of heart, even though it was only slight, left her mother dumbfounded, and she looked after her daughter as she vanished up the stairs and to her room.

"Goodnight…" She called after her, her voice trailing off somewhat.

After a few moments relief crept through Dyra's chest and a slight smile touched her lips. Pushing herself to her feet, she wandered through into the lounge and collapsed onto the faded leather settee that sat back up against the wall closest to the kitchen.

She felt suddenly weightless and exhausted, as at least a little of the heavy anxiety that she had carried with her fell suddenly from her shoulders.

Naturally, Jen did eventually find her way up onto the rooftop, crouching and locating the spot where she was most comfortable on sea view side.

This time though she didn't take her Walkman with her.

She had even tried briefly to fall asleep in bed, but she had not had much success.

Her thoughts still raced and her body still felt the after effects of Deacon…

"What happened?" Clare asked her, sliding carefully along the slanted rooftop in her plain, white dress, luminous in the night, crouching slowly to sit by her younger sister.

"I'm sorry I didn't come to meet you…" Jen apologised immediately, misunderstanding Clare's question completely.

"No, not that…" Clare replied, waving off her apology as if she'd accepted it before it had even been made. "I meant, what happened with Deacon?"

"What? Oh, erm…I…I don't know." Jen stumbled, phased even at the sheer mention of his name.

"See!?" Clare exclaimed then, her voice carrying perhaps further than she'd intended through the dark night from the rooftop.

But she didn't care, and it didn't matter anyway.

No one would have heard her.

Jen flushed again, and Clare saw it even in the dim light.

"That! See! There!" She exclaimed again. That's exactly what I mean!" She chuckled, pointing at Jen's furious blushing. "Even just his name!? Really!?"

"Stop it!" Jen begged, covering her ears and burying her face, though of course that made no difference whatsoever.

"How's he done this!?" Clare laughed then. "You even wanted him to kiss you didn't you!? Admit it!" Clare jested seriously. "You've never wanted that before in your life!"

"He…I…I really don't know…" Jen floundered helplessly.

She had no answers to give.

"Jenny…" Clare said then, smirking, raising her eyebrows and tilting her head at her younger sister.

Jen looked her older sister in the eyes and knew in an instant exactly what she was thinking.

"Don't say it…" Jen warned, though there was a pleading tone in her voice too.

But it mattered not. The words were already on Clare's tongue.

Jen knew what they were anyway.

Either way, regardless, there was no way she could have escaped them.

Her older sister's voice rang true like bells echoing out over the vast shoreline.

"You've fallen in love."

Sleep came quickly when Jen eventually crept back down into her bedroom, but her mind did not rest, and all through the night her crazed, muddled up thoughts turned into exhausting dreams that left her feeling even more drained than before.

Jen saw herself in her dreams on Memoria Lane. She clocked the street name sign straight away. Not that she'd needed to check it, for this was the street where she always met Clare from work, and she recognised it immediately.

The streetlights were bright, but few and far between, and lit lonesome yellow spotlights all the way along the lane for as far as she could see in either direction.

Trees and shrubs and bushes lined the narrow lane on both sides, broken here and there by gaps of darkness that shrouded around harrowingly.

Usually there would have been cars flitting past, crossing paths here and there for brief, fleeting moments where the lane occasionally widened. There were crossing places, after all, but here, now, in her dream, Jen's mind was frantic and silent all at once, and no cars passed by that night.

Next, Jen found herself walking along the lane, meandering through the darkness of the night, crossing paths every hundred paces or so with one of the yellowish spotlights. The cold did not affect her, even though she was only wearing jeans and a T-shirt, for of course that would only have been her mind playing tricks on her.

Although, what else are minds for if not for playing tricks?

Jen's was certainly having a field day.

She rounded a corner that appeared from nowhere, still following the same lane, and continued on down towards the shop where Clare worked. It wasn't quite in view yet, but no matter how far she walked, it never got any closer.

Regardless, she continued, knowing it would eventually appear. Either that, or beforehand she would meet her older sister on her way home from work. They usually crossed paths in the middle somewhere.

There was no real sense of time in her dream, but if she had to guess, Jen would have likely deduced that far too long had passed, and that Clare would usually had found her by now.

Perhaps she'd finished late?

Suddenly a rustle off to the side of the lane startled her, and Jen's attention focused in on the blackness intently. She couldn't see a thing, but the noise sounded again, forcing fear to course through her body.

Shouting for help, her voice carried far and wide through the endless night.

But nobody came to her aid.

Then, still staring in terror at the darkness before her, visible only barely by the dim reaches of the yellow light from the streetlamps, Jen saw a silhouette detach itself from the trees and bushes and undergrowth.

It was the figure of a man.

All of a sudden she was petrified, and desperately yearned to run. But, hard as she tried, her legs would not budge.

As much as she willed, her body would not listen.

It was as if she had been trapped there endlessly, unable to escape, for a very long time.

The figure approached, seeming to glide above the ground in the faint light, hazy and unclear, and as it moved, Jen's stomach turned and lurched in terror.

But then, as the figure continued to draw ever closer, her feelings stirred anew.

She suddenly felt alive and renewed, invigorated afresh for the first time. And as the silhouette separated itself from the shadows, breaking away from the darkness, her heart lifted and her spirit soared as she saw who in fact it was.

Deacon.

He didn't speak.

And Jen couldn't.

She was tongue tied again.

A chill wind whipped between them, but it was not cold.

The streetlamps dimmed and blackened, but still they could see.

Jen was only human, and a barely functioning one at that, yet, now she felt as though she could fly.

Albatross

It was as if she was stood back in the doorway to The Rusty Oak, seeing Deacon for the very first time, and she imagined it would always feel like that.

At the very least, she hoped it would.

Ross Turner

Sunlit Chorus

Dyra awoke slowly, hearing the murmuring of voices in the distance that doesn't quite startle you to consciousness, but instead rouses you gradually and leaves you groggy and confused. She blinked awake a few times, groaning inaudibly as she did so.

It was only as her senses awakened, sluggishly, one by one, that Dyra was able to gain any sense of focus whatsoever.

Light streamed in through the crack between her curtains, blinding her momentarily, but that wasn't what grabbed her attention the most.

Straining to hear as best she could, once she'd finally realised what it was that had awoken her, Dyra cocked her ear to one side and focused intently. But it was no use. The sound was too far away and the walls were too thick. All she could hear were murmurs. She couldn't make out any words.

Rising from beneath her quilt and swivelling round to the side, dropping her legs off the edge of the bed, she stood up and reached for her thick, grey dressing gown, pulling it on over her nightclothes.

She silently opened her bedroom door and stepped slowly out onto the landing. To her right was the stairway leading up to Jen's bedroom, and to her left were the stairs leading down to the hall. Out on the landing she could hear more clearly the murmurs that had stirred her, and now she could tell that they were indeed only one voice.

Jennifer's.

Pacing down onto the stairs, she moved gradually, pausing for a moment as her gaze briefly caught the picture of the three of them: herself, Clare, and Jen, all stood outside the house when they'd first moved in.

Dyra stared at it blankly for a moment, totally lost in thought, her expression unreadable.

Eventually moving on, she continued to descend the stairs, and Jennifer's voice became clear enough to make out the occasional word, but still hers was the only voice Dyra could hear.

And then it all went quiet, and there was not a sound to be heard.

Dyra pressed on, growing only more confused.

But then, all of a sudden, just as she reached the penultimate step, about three seconds from turning the corner and entering the kitchen, the loud banging and scraping of pots and pans startled her, and it was all she could do to keep herself from crying out in shock.

Her hand came up to her mouth to conceal any escaping sound, and even as it did, she heard Jennifer's voice again, clear as day this time, and the sound brought tears to her mother's eyes.

Her youngest daughter burst out in song once more, perfectly in tune, singing a melody that Dyra knew all too well.

Jennifer, so troubled of late, was singing a love song! And not just any love song, but in fact, the very song that Dyra had chosen for her wedding day.

Her stomach churned and her spirits lifted enormously.

Cooking and singing!

The tears that had been welling in her eyes streamed instantly down her cheeks, and Jen's mother retreated back upstairs, just as silently as she had come.

Feeling herself go weak at the knees, she slumped back against her bedroom door and slid down to the floor.

Great surges of relief flooded through her in enormous waves.

Perhaps everything would be alright after all…

It was another ten or fifteen minutes before Dyra had dressed and composed herself enough to venture downstairs once more.

She heard Jen's voice again, this time even before she'd made it halfway down the staircase, and she was still singing, though now it wasn't Dyra's wedding song, and she managed to just about hold herself together.

"Good morning sweetheart." She greeted her youngest daughter with a broad smile as she entered.

Jen was wearing jeans and a T-shirt, as per usual, but there was something about her that morning that made it look like the sunbeams streaming in through the window had been cast for the sole purpose of illuminating her every flowing movement.

"Morning mom!" Jen replied, breaking tune for barely a moment, tending expertly to scrambled egg with one hand and lightly buttering toast with the other.

She had always been a marvel to watch in the kitchen, Dyra thought to herself, as she observed Jen dance and juggle and sing in a display of great skill.

It was most definitely something that cannot be taught, but instead simply something that is learned only through a love of cooking.

"What's the occasion?" Jen's mother asked, pulling a chair up at the table and pouring herself a glass of orange juice that Jen had already laid out ready, along with placemats, cutlery, and a variety of seasonings.

"Does there have to be an occasion?" Jen asked merrily, breaking her melody and casting a quick smile over her shoulder, before picking up her song exactly where she left off, without so much as breaking a note.

Dyra still didn't know what was happening, which clearly was something, but if she was brutally honest, at that particular point in time, she didn't really care. She was just overjoyed to see her daughter smile again.

Within minutes breakfast was served. Eggs and sausage and bacon, fried bread, beans, toast, hash browns, and even fried tomatoes graced the table that day, and much to her mother's delight, for the first time in months, Jen tucked well in to the lot.

Her daughter seemed to glow in the morning light as it filtered in through the open windows, and birds filled the gap in Jen's beautiful song as she ate, bursting with a dawn chorus of their own.

"So what are your plans today, sweetheart?" Dyra asked, wiping her mouth with a serviette. "Are you working?"

Jen was mid-swig of orange juice and swallowed before she spoke.

"Later…" She replied, nodding. "I'm going into town first…"

"Oh, really?" Her mother questioned, intrigued, and Jen nodded again.

"I'm going to buy a new dress." She explained.

"Really!?" Her mother exclaimed, in perhaps more of a shocked tone than she'd intended. "And is there no occasion for this either?" She asked slyly, eyeing her youngest daughter with an unconcealed smirk.

"I just feel like it…" Jen lied, though she failed in turn to hide a grin of her own.

"Alright then…" Dyra conceded, not wanting to push Jen too far. Especially when things seemed to be improving so.

Clare appeared behind their mother then from seemingly nowhere, and she threw Jen a smug grin that spoke a thousand and more words.

Most prominently though, it said, 'I told you so. You're in love.'

Jen smirked, but ignored her older sister, clearing away the plates from breakfast and starting the washing up.

Aside from everything that had happened, she couldn't help but be excited.

Perhaps, just perhaps, Clare was right…

The morning outside proved to be a glorious one, and the perfectly clear blue sky, broken by only the odd wisp of brilliantly white cloud here and there, shone vividly above. The lanes were quiet and though the town was a fair distance away to walk, Jen felt revitalised anew, and decided it would be a waste not to enjoy the day.

"You should have told mom!" Clare teased her playfully as they strolled.

"No!" Jen exclaimed in retort. "I can't tell her!"

"Oh go onnnn!" Clare pushed.

"I don't want her to know!" Jen replied adamantly.

"I'll tell her if you don't!" Clare stated mischievously.

"You can't…" Jen commented.

"Wanna bet?" Clare asked slyly.

"Yes, actually. I do." Jen asserted, finding new confidence in herself that she thought she'd lost long ago. "You can't…I won't let you…"

Town was busy, and following their little spate, Clare and Jen hadn't really spoken the rest of the way.

It wasn't really much of a shopping hub, for in the grand scheme of things, it was little more than an oversized village. However, it was where the vast majority of the locals went for their everyday needs: clothes, food and the like, and so, as expected, there were enough people there, and enough people who knew her, for Jen's unexpected appearance to be noted.

Many who hadn't seen or spoken to her for months stopped to say hello and asked how she was, and were all pleasantly surprised when they got a conversation out of her, and a happy one at that.

Before long, Clare and Jen had been in four different shops, Jen had tried on nine different dresses and, having been heavily critiqued by her grumpy older sister, still hadn't made a decision.

They had virtually exhausted all their options, and still, as seemed to always be the case, in perhaps more ways than anyone could possibly ever know, Clare was forever casting doubt into Jen's thoughts.

"Oh will you just make up your mind!" Clare demanded, exasperated, throwing her arms up in the air.

"Can you just leave me alone for two minutes!?" Jen practically begged of her sister.

Onlookers walked past with concerned, confused expressions on their faces, especially those who had spoken to Jen only an hour or two ago, when she had seemed so happy and carefree.

"Fine!" Clare cried, raising her voice so much that Jen visibly winced. "If you don't want me, that's just fine!"

"No…Clare…" Jen started, but it was too late.

In an instant, Clare was gone.

Jen could only watch as in one moment she was there beside her, and in the next she wasn't, fading away into the distance between the crowds.

Jen sighed as she watched her sister go, and felt the eyes of all those around upon her much more keenly that she would have liked.

Desperate to divert from the attention, and barely able to control the emotions welling up inside of her from the knowledge of what she'd just done, intentionally or not, she turned and headed immediately back into the nearest shop.

Moments later she found herself locked in a changing room with three dresses that she couldn't even have told you the colours of, her head buried in her hands and her chest heaving.

However, for some reason, after a few more minutes, she had recovered considerably, and it seemed that the argument had taken much less out of her than she'd originally thought.

Only ten minutes later, now making wholly her own decisions, Jen had made up her mind: a sleek, black dress lined with lace and a handful of tastefully placed sequins.

By the time she left the shop, already wearing her new purchase, though still with her trainers on admittedly, which looked for the most part quite comical, Jen was feeling strangely free and uplifted.

Still, people were eyeing her cautiously as she walked by, but at that point she didn't care.

Now she had only one thing in mind, and one destination in view.

Lust

"Do you really think he'll be there?" Clare asked, seeing as always directly into the centre of everything Jen thought, knowing in a heartbeat the real reason for the dress and for Jen's immediate visit to the beach.

"I didn't think you'd still be here…" Jen commented honestly, glancing across at her older sister walking beside her still. But the response she got was not exactly what she was expecting.

"You can't get rid of me." Clare replied, quite seriously, with something even of a sinister tone to her voice. "I'll be here forever…"

Jen nodded, but didn't reply. Her sister's words were true, she knew that.

But, considering the circumstances, they were nearly impossible to swallow.

Clare, of course, was right.

She couldn't be wrong.

Soon the beach was in sight.

The skies were still clear, though perhaps a little cloudier than earlier in the morning. A salty wind cut at Jen's exposed legs, unused to being open to the elements.

Clare strolled beside her younger sister still. Neither of them spoke now, and she followed Jen as she led her down across the pebbles covering the top half of the beach, just off the path, instead of immediately onto the rocks as per usual.

Albatross

Passing over the shingles, sunlight dancing across her face, Jen took off her shoes as she reached the divide between the pebbles and the beach. She stepped forward, burying her feet into the soft, oddly warm sand, and felt it slip and slide blissfully between her toes.

She had been on this beach virtually every day for the past year, and yet in all that time she hadn't once enjoyed it like she was now.

"Jenny…" Clare started, but Jen knew exactly what she was going to ask, and she sighed deeply, knowing that her sister's words were altogether a possibility. "What are you going to do if he doesn't come?"

But then, as if on cue, to answer Clare's question, and indeed even her own, Jen caught the flicker of movement out of the corner of her eye.

She turned to face the figure that had appeared across the way, on the sand. But when she laid eyes upon it, it was not who she had expected.

It was not Deacon.

It was the albatross.

He had landed barely a dozen feet from where Jen stood, his vast wingspan casting an enormous shadow over the golden sands.

Jen looked up, confused.

The water was so green, and yet so blue at the same time, that it only reminded Jen of something else entirely.

Even the rocks in the distance upon which she usually sat glistened, wet and sparkling under the face of the sun.

And her albatross looked on curiously.

He didn't look quite as sad today, and instead looked a little more satisfied with what he saw.

As much as she knew he was a solitary creature, Jen couldn't help but feel the majestic bird looking on at her now seemed thoughtful, considerate, and had many other characteristics of a human; a decent human that is.

One that actually cares.

With that thought, Jen looked across to her sister, only to find that she was glancing between the two of them, and her expression was a most puzzling one. It was profoundly clear and vastly indecipherable all at once.

The albatross spread his vast wings, flapping them only a single time in an enormous movement, taking to the skies, and casting a massive shadow over Jen.

But suddenly, in his place, out of nowhere, stood Deacon.

The instant Jen laid eyes upon him, smiling his cheeky grin, she went weak at the knees. Without a sound he walked over towards her, and as he approached, Jen caught yet more movement out of the corner of her eye.

Glancing across, she saw Clare once again walking off into the distance, disappearing without a trace.

In that moment, Jen didn't even really know how it felt to see her older sister walk away.

It was something she had been dreading for a very long time now.

"Good afternoon." Deacon greeted her, bowing his head slightly, and his voice like rough velvet made certain that she knew exactly how she felt right then.

He wore brown board shorts and shoes, and a red collared shirt that was not quite buttoned all the way to the top or the bottom, which for some reason drove Jen nuts, though she had no idea really why.

She realised then that she'd not even noticed what he'd been wearing the night before, but he most certainly didn't look out of place now, and her heart skipped joyously.

Suddenly racing, beating furiously against her chest, Jen could feel her heartbeat in her ears, and the impulsive desire to leap forward and lock her lips to Deacon's returned.

The feeling was infinitely stronger than before, almost overwhelming her, and she was forced to beat down the desire with more control than she had ever exercised in her whole life.

"Good afternoon…" She replied, managing to get her words out without stammering, but only barely.

"You look lovely." Deacon complimented her.

"Thank you…" Jen replied, blushing, naturally.

Deacon turned up one corner of his mouth, looking at Jen with deep affection in his eyes.

An entirely new range of emotions flushed through Jen's body. Her heart never ceased its manic racing, shaking her ribs and shuddering her every breath. Her palms burned, her stomach churned, and her gaze flitted between Deacon's eyes, his shirt, his chest, and everything else…

Something burned in Jen's chest and pushed fiercely at her. It was something that she didn't know; something that she had only felt for the first time since meeting Deacon.

What was it?

She didn't know.

She just wanted him.

She needed him.

It was a burning desire she was barely able to keep in check.

She was lust filled and desperate. But for what, exactly, she didn't quite yet know. Although, she knew what she wanted in that particular instant, for it was standing right in front of her.

Deacon tucked his hands into his back pockets, taking a deep breath as he did so, and Jen bit her bottom lip achingly.

Finally, after what felt like a lifetime of silence, though by no means was it awkward, at last Deacon spoke again.

"Will you be here again tomorrow?" He asked Jen, pulling one hand from his pocket and brushing her exposed arm lightly, though for no real reason.

Where she had felt the cold before, Jen flushed even more furiously, and unexplored heat continued to surge through her.

"I'm…I…" She started, but Deacon's smile widened and spread to a slight chuckle, forcing her shyness out.

Jen could have sworn she saw the albatross pass overhead yet again, but when she looked up, he was nowhere in sight.

Deacon followed her gaze curiously, but the skies were empty.

"Looks like he's gone…" Deacon noted whimsically.

"What? How do you…?" Jen questioned, shocked.

Deacon didn't answer with words. He only smiled shrewdly and winked cheekily at Jen.

Her gaze dropped and, of course, she continued to blush terribly.

"No, I won't…I'm working at The Rusty Oak…" Jen finally managed to answer. "I'll be done just after half four…"

"Well then!" Deacon exclaimed suddenly. "And perchance, my dear, might you be free past the hour of five, tomorrow evening?" He asked, gesturing extravagantly and bowing slightly, splaying his arms out to his sides, though smirking cheekily up at Jen as he did so.

She couldn't take much more of this.

He was reducing her to a flushed, infatuated wreck.

But as much as she couldn't stand it, she loved it, and she never wanted it to end.

"I am…" She replied, grinning uncontrollably herself, praying he would say next what she hoped was coming.

"In which case…" He declared, holding one hand to his chest and brushing Jen's arm again with the other. "My dear Jen, I shall pick you up from The Rusty Oak at five tomorrow evening!"

"Where are we going?" Jen asked, of course.

"Ah!" He replied mysteriously. "That would be telling!"

"How will I know what to wear?" She asked, nervous and excited all at once.

"Just bring a jacket so you're warm enough…" Deacon replied, smiling with his eyes.

"Okay…" She responded, unsure and certain all at once.

"Are you at The Oak today?" He asked then, flicking his wrist to check his watch. Jen hadn't even noticed he'd been wearing one, and saw that it was a silver and chrome device, very neat with a well-worn brown leather strap.

"Yes…" Jen replied, though she desperately didn't want to leave yet.

"Would you permit me to accompany you to work?" He offered then, holding out his hand in a very gallant manner.

Jen nodded numbly, and within a whirlwind of an instant they headed off, the sand whooshing beneath Jen's feet and between her toes, and crunching and grinding beneath Deacon's brown leather shoes.

She slipped her shoes back on as they crossed the gravel, brushing the sand from her feet, and Deacon held his hand out to steady her as she did so. Jen took it gratefully, but then, as they stepped back up onto the path, and soon enough found themselves once again on the lanes, heading towards The Rusty Oak, she desperately wanted him to hold her hand again as they walked.

Though she was unsure exactly why, for they had never seemed so before, the spaces between her fingers felt empty, and undoubtedly his would fit between them perfectly.

But Jen was too shy, and too embarrassed to say anything, and almost before she knew it The Rusty Oak came into view, as several clouds parted overhead, following the winds.

They were walking in silence now, but he was still smiling that cheeky smile that seemed, for reasons unknown, to drive her crazy.

Then Jen spotted her sister out of the corner of her eye, stood by the entrance to The Rusty Oak as they approached.

Clare had been waiting for her, and by the wide smirk on her face, clearly she knew exactly the internal turmoil that Jen was struggling with.

'Just do it!' Her older sister mouthed silently to her from across the lane.

Jen shook her head and gritted her teeth in indecision.

It was now or never.

They were almost at The Rusty Oak.

She was running out of time.

At no point over the last year had she stuck her neck on the line for anything; she hadn't had the courage.

She hadn't taken a risk for so long. She didn't even know if she still knew how. But now, for the first time in far too long, this felt like it was worth it.

Deacon was worth it.

Screw it.

They were already so close together that their arms brushed more occasionally than not, and neither of them made a move to change that.

Suddenly, Jen felt her fingers interlocking with Deacon's, and they slipped together so easily, weaving together so perfectly, that it felt like the most natural thing in the world.

They held hands for barely thirty seconds before they reached the tall, stone inn looming before them that was The Rusty Oak.

Somehow, in what felt like only a moment, they had bypassed Clare, leaving her far behind, and found themselves stood beneath the giant metal oak tree itself, out in the back garden.

It was quiet, though it would undoubtedly be busy later, but at least for now they had some privacy.

Laura's head popped round the corner, having seen Jen slip past and out into the garden, wondering if she was alright.

She stopped, however, when she saw that Jen had company, smiling and holding hands with a stranger that Laura did not know.

Her face lit up and her heart leapt for them, overjoyed, and she rushed back inside so as not to disturb.

Jen did not see her.

Deacon did, out of the corner of his eye. But then, he saw everything with his all-encompassing gaze, as Jen was quickly coming to realise.

He ignored the fact however, for his focus was entirely on her.

He still held Jen's hand, gently and tightly all at once, and her fingers locked between his pulsed with her racing heartbeat. Deacon could feel it vibrating against his palm, and he cast his cheeky smile upon Jen again, sending her weak at the knees, his face barely inches from hers.

What Deacon did not see, however, somehow, was Clare, sat directly behind him, watching the pair of them with an expression cast across her face that was completely unreadable.

She looked as though she was made of stone, but at the same time so fluid and fragile that she might disappear at any moment.

But Deacon was oblivious to her presence.

"Have a good night…" He breathed to Jen, his voice not even a whisper.

Jen wanted to say something, to reply, anything. But unable to speak once again, she merely nodded.

Her eyes were locked on the bluey green pools of his gaze, which reminded her so of the colour of the ocean earlier that afternoon.

They drew her in, and she was powerless to resist.

She so desperately wanted him.

But it was bound to never be that easy, and he smiled and melted her once more.

"I'll pick you up tomorrow night then…" He breathed again, moving his lips yet even closer, but still not quite touching her.

"Okay…" She just about managed, almost choking on the word as she forced sound from her tongue.

And then, with that, he placed his hand slowly on the back of her neck, kissed her tenderly on the forehead, and he was gone.

He looked round only once, quite purposefully, and Jen hung for what felt like forever in limbo.

Her one hand remained unconsciously outstretched, watching him go, longing desperately for him to return.

Anticipation

More often than not for the duration of that evening, and indeed the entire day to follow, Jen's seemingly ceaseless humming broke into songs of countless different keys. Her voice, unused properly for so long, burst out joyously, finally released from its captive slumber.

Needless to say, everybody noticed.

The kitchen in The Rusty Oak that day and the next was filled with chorus upon verse upon chorus, and Geoff and Jen waltzed and worked and hummed and sang to their hearts' content, and for a time it was almost as if nothing had ever changed.

Their energy seeped out from between the hot stoves and infected the free house uncontrollably, and the atmosphere that night was unrivalled. In all the years Laura had lived and worked at The Oak, she had never witnessed such a thing, and it brought joy to her heart and a tear to her eye.

Nonetheless, for young Jen that twenty four hours seemed to take an age and even longer to pass, for she was simply marking time, waiting for the return of Deacon.

Even as Jen plated her sister's sweet, this time a banana split, adorned with lashings of ice cream and sauce, and left it in the fridge for her, her thoughts were constantly set upon the mysterious young man.

She grabbed her things to head home, a little dazed and in a world of her own as she moved.

Her walk home was silent and subdued. Clare walked close beside her, though she didn't say a word either.

When they got home they climbed briefly up to the rooftop of Keepers Cottage, clambering in a crablike fashion, invisible silhouettes blacked out against the skyline.

Continuing to sit in silence and gaze out across the coast, Jen glanced briefly across at Clare, highlighted in the darkness. Her beautiful sister's expression was indecipherable, but then, as always, Jen knew what she was thinking.

Before too long however, dropping back down through into her room, Jen curled up in her bed, wrapping herself amidst the quilt so long unused, and fell into sleep far too deep for dreams.

The following day could not come quickly enough, but the hours of darkness whipped by faster than they had done in months. Soon enough dawn broke out gloriously over the misty Welsh coastline, and Jen rose with eagerness wrapped about her, just as her warm quilt had been all throughout the hours of blackness.

Breakfast was a blur of heat and steam and eggs and bacon, littered here and there with toast and butter. But Jen's mind was not on food.

Her mother, Dyra, looked on thoughtfully as her daughter sung and danced around the kitchen, not concentrating even in the slightest on the food she was preparing, though it still all came out perfectly.

Already Dyra could see that Jen looked healthier, stronger, happier, and more content. But she knew that, although the fact that Jen was now eating again was partly responsible, there was something else going on too.

What it was exactly, she couldn't put her finger on, and she was afraid to ask, save ruining it. And so, besides that, she had no other way of knowing.

She decided she would just have to stay in the dark a little while longer.

For now, at least, she was content with the fact that her youngest daughter seemed to be drastically improving.

"One egg, or two?" Jen asked then, barely even breaking note in her song, picking up exactly where she left off.

This time she sang a low, meaningful, emotional melody; it was something her mother had never before heard from her, and once again Dyra felt tears begin to well in her eyes.

"Just the one please, sweetheart..." She replied, her voice trailing off. She was somewhat eager to lead into a question, though none followed, and Jen didn't ask.

Soon enough breakfast was served, and seemingly even sooner came the time for Jen to leave for work, though her mother was sure she was leaving much earlier than necessary.

Jen knew that it didn't matter if she arrived early at The Rusty Oak, five o'clock would not come around any faster.

Still, it can't hurt to try.

The sky that day was overcast to begin with, though the sun broke through the clouds every now and then as the morning wore on into early afternoon.

Between walking to work, and waltzing and singing around the kitchens, Jen barely noticed the slow passage of the day.

But then also, at the same time, she was aware of nothing else, as the seconds and minutes and hours laboured slowly by, taunting her with their every moment.

She checked her watch again for the hundredth time: seventeen minutes past three.

Pursing her lips, Jen pressed on, knowing that all things, both good and bad, eventually come around.

"What are you waiting for?" Geoff asked her, his voice melting through the air between the sounds of boiling kettles, spitting pans and whirring ovens.

Jen glanced over to him quickly. He didn't even look up, and simply continued chopping vegetables, but clearly her nervous impatience hadn't gone unnoticed.

"I, erm…I…" Jen started, attempting in vain to come up with a decent enough lie.

But Geoff only smiled and shook his head slightly.

"So, what's the lucky guy's name?" He asked, chuckling as he spoke.

"What? I…" Jen almost choked, getting more tongue tied by the second. "How…"

"Jen…" Geoff said then quite seriously, placing his knife down and turning to face her. "I have three daughters, with four years between each of them…"

Jen nodded, but didn't speak to reply.

"And every one of them…" He continued. "Had exactly that same look about them before their first dates…" He finished, waving his open hand towards Jen's nervous, expectant, and terrified expression.

"And how did they go?" Jen asked, smiling ruefully, knowing know she couldn't have hidden it from Geoff even if she'd wanted to.

"The first two, splendidly. In fact, they're both married now to those same guys…"

Jen smiled.

"And the third?" She asked then.

"Horribly!" Geoff laughed, cackling evilly and turning back to his vegetables as if the whole thing had been hilarious. "Completely crashed and burned! Went up in flames! Might even still be smouldering!"

"Thanks…" Jen responded dryly, even as Geoff continued his chuckling.

"I'm kidding! I'm kidding!" He quickly backtracked, though wry humour still hung on his words.

"It went well?" Jen asked again, her words hopeful that he had indeed been joking.

"What? Oh, no, no, it was genuinely horrible…" Geoff shot her down, this time with a more serious and sincere note to his tone, as if it hadn't been quite so hilarious.

"Great…" Jen receded.

"What time?" Geoff asked then.

Jen checked her watch again.

"Almost half three." Jen replied.

"No! You fool!" Geoff burst into laughter again then. "What time's your date!?"

"Oh!" Jen replied, blushing and dropping her head slightly, though admittedly she cracked a smile. "Five…"

"And where are you going?" Geoff enquired curiously.

Jen looked over at him as he glanced up again from his vegetables.

"I have no idea…" She admitted, and he only smiled in response, nodding ever so slightly and in a very mysterious fashion, as if he knew something that she most certainly did not.

Just as she knew it would, the time eventually neared five o'clock, and Jen felt in every way, shape, and form, unprepared.

Though she wore the same sleek, black dress that she had bought only the day before, and held a jacket folded over her one arm, as Deacon had requested, she felt her nerves tingle and shudder as the hour approached.

"Any sign yet?" Geoff asked, walking over from the kitchen on his break, drying his hands with a tea towel.

Jen sat side on to the main door, glancing over occasionally, sipping a glass of water.

"Not yet…" She replied.

"It's still early, isn't it?" He asked, checking the time himself.

Just after ten to five.

"Mmm…" Jen nodded.

Suddenly then though, Geoff's expression changed and he practically beamed at her.

"Have a wonderful time." He offered, and retreated back to the bar where Laura stood watching also.

Jen rose and turned towards the door, and laid eyes immediately upon exactly what she'd been waiting so impatiently for.

"Good evening, Jen…" Deacon greeted her, bowing his head slightly as he spoke, though not once taking his eyes from her.

Jen's gaze swept up and down the mysterious Deacon in an instant, and quite obviously so, taking in everything that she possibly could. Though, undoubtedly, it would still never be enough.

He wore pressed black trousers with very thin, almost unnoticeable grey stripes running vertically up and down them, and buffed black shoes. His collared shirt was black also, very smart and well fitted, with not a mark or crease to be seen that didn't belong there. His hair seemed longer than Jen remembered, though it was cut very short on the sides, and he smiled welcomingly at her.

Although he was dressed so sharply, he looked relaxed, casual even, and Jen felt completely lost even just in his presence.

"Deacon…" Was all that she managed, once she had finished sweeping her eyes over him longingly.

He laughed slightly, and one corner of his mouth turned up seemingly higher than the other.

Having already looked Jen up and down a hundred times, even still he did so. As far as he could see, which was quite a long way to be sure, for there was rarely anything he ever missed with his keen gaze, she was flawless.

"Shall we?" He asked her then, offering her his outstretched hand.

She took it without a word and followed him out into the fading afternoon light.

Deacon flashed a smile to Geoff and Laura, and briefly waved them goodbye. They both turned away, Laura blushing and Geoff chuckling, for as discreet as they might have been trying to keep their watching's, Deacon had spotted them in an instant.

Jen smiled and laughed slightly.

"How do you do that?" She asked him, just as he held the door open for her and the chilled air rushed in from outside.

"You'll see…" He replied mysteriously.

Jen looked up at him with a questioning frown.

"I'll show you…"

On Top of the World

During the car journey Jen felt as if she was daydreaming the whole way. Deacon drove a sleek, black Mercedes that looked far too expensive for anyone their age to be able to afford.

Jen hadn't been driven by anybody since getting into Geoff's banged up old death trap of a car, and, especially in comparison, Deacon's driving was absolutely flawless, and infinitely smoother.

Inside the car the seats were all leather, the dashboard was dark mahogany, and every surface was scrupulously clean.

The sun was dipping its head lower and lower in the sky, and beginning to throw huge, arcing orange and yellow strips out across the vast expanse of darkening blue above. Jen's eyes wandered over the sight before her endlessly. However, she most certainly allowed her eyes to wander to the driver in the seat next to her, every now and then, or perhaps even a little more frequently than that.

Deacon pretended not to notice, and instead focused on the road, but Jen knew he saw her every time she looked. Nonetheless, he made no motion to stop her, and in turn she made less and less effort to keep her wandering gaze inconspicuous.

"Where are we going?" She eventually asked, breaking the casual silence that had fallen over them.

"We're almost there…" Deacon replied, glancing across to her briefly and smiling.

His response didn't really answer her question at all, but butterflies stirred in Jen's stomach and her cheeks flushed pink.

Finally, as they turned down a narrow lane off the main road, squeezing between the trees on either side as the sun cast orange beams down upon the forest, Jen at last saw what Deacon had planned for their evening.

Emerging from between the illuminated trunks, Jen's mouth dropped open and her eyes flicked between Deacon's quirky smile and the sight she beheld before her.

Attached with rope to what looked like an enormous wicker basket, a giant, half inflated balloon, the top of it red and the bottom blue, grew and expanded and rose slowly above the roaring tongue of flame exploding up from a metal burner.

Deacon pulled the car up about two dozen feet or so away from the basket, within which a man was teasing the balloon up higher and higher with the dancing flame.

In an instant Jen's door opened, startling her, for she had been so engrossed she hadn't even heard Deacon get out of the car.

"Are you ready?" He asked her, holding out his hand for Jen once more, and as she looked up at him, his cheeky smile sent the butterflies that had been in her stomach cascading throughout her entire body; down every vein and into every crevice they flew.

"Are we…?" She started, swivelling her legs round slowly, taking his hand and rising from the leather seat. "Really…? Are we going…?"

Albatross

Deacon laughed gently again.

"Yes, Jen." He replied, linking his right arm with her left and taking her hand smoothly. "We really are."

Jen didn't say another word as she stood and watched the hot air balloon inflate gradually to its full size, hand in hand and arm in arm with Deacon. When it was at its full height the balloon stood about a hundred feet tall and Jen gawped up at it in all its splendour, like a child seeing something amazing for the very first time.

"Deacon!" The man who had been toying with the burner and inflating the balloon greeted him, his voice serious, but mischievous and roguish all at once.

Although he was an older chap, he practically threw himself out of the huge wicker basket, landing perfectly on his feet, thudding into the ground, and skipped across the grass towards them.

His face was rugged and his hair was perfectly white: short and messy. He wore what looked to be a rich, blue doublet over a ruffled white shirt, as though he was from a time long forgotten, and his high, black boots reached almost to the knees of his dark blue jeans.

Much the curious character.

"Good evening Grimm." Deacon replied, bowing his head slightly, as he always seemed to.

And if this so called Grimm had been wearing a hat, and could have tipped it to Deacon in return, Jen was almost certain he would have done.

"Jen…" Deacon said then, looking down to meet her gaze. "This is my dear friend, Walter Grimmway."

"Ever the gentleman!" Walter exclaimed, motioning to Deacon exuberantly, his every action seemingly exaggerated and flamboyant. "Please, my dear, call me Grimm!"

"My pleasure…" Jen greeted this strangely energetic, elderly man, scrawny and full all at once.

She didn't know quite what to make of him.

"Oh no! The pleasure is all mine!" Grimm replied then, spreading his arms wide and taking several paces backward. "Welcome! My friends! Allow me to introduce you to the Duchess!"

"The Duchess?" Jen whispered to Deacon, still clutching his hand tightly, and Deacon squeezed her fingers affectionately in return.

"It's what he calls the balloon." Deacon explained, whispering also in reply.

Grimm began to dance around the enormous wicker basket, seeming to check that everything was in order, pulling here and there on the ropes before jumping back into the giant hamper and leaning this way and that beneath the burner.

"He's a bit eccentric…" Deacon admitted. "But you get used to it."

"Right then me hearties!" Grimm cried then, launching himself up onto the side of the basket, clutching one of the ropes in his left hand like a pirate looking out across the ocean, as his head bobbed precariously close to the burner. "Are ye ready to set sail into the sunset!?"

And before they even had chance to answer, he dropped back into the basket and sent the burner roaring into life once again, and the Duchess began to tug fiercely on the ropes holding it to the ground.

Jen looked up at Deacon once more, this time rather sceptically.

"Okay…" He confessed, chuckling. "You don't get used to it, but he does grow on you…"

The skies were clear and Jen could see for miles every way she looked.

To the West lay the ocean stretching right out to the horizon, and in every other direction for as far as she could see the rolling Welsh hills and mountains gave way dramatically before them.

By now the sunset was in its full glory and far away over the ocean the sun cast its last light of the day across the rippling waves. Great arms of orange reached out in every direction, and the sight drew even Deacon's all-seeing gaze to focus upon it.

Grimm had been so eccentric and loud and enthusiastic before, but now, as they rose higher and higher into the sky, he was silent and subdued, and apparently entirely contented by the view laid out before him.

In fact, thankfully, Jen barely even noticed he was there, as Deacon took her into his encompassing embrace.

"It's amazing…" Jen breathed, her voice barely even loud enough for Deacon to hear.

He did though, of course, and he smiled warmly in return.

Jen leant back against his strong chest and he wrapped his arms forwards around her. Though her jacket was draped over her shoulders, Jen felt Deacon's warmth keeping the chill of their dizzying height at bay.

The light from the sunset cast a final warming glow across their faces, as Jen, moving without even realising, turned to face Deacon, his arms still enveloping her protectively. She crept her hands up his body and over his shoulders, running her fingers lightly through his hair as she did so, and he smiled in the way that only he did, turning her legs to jelly.

Neither on them spoke, but then again, they didn't need to.

Jen's gaze was lost in Deacon's and he pulled her body close to his, gently, but at the same time longingly. And in that moment, overwhelmed with desire and lust and desperate wanting, Jen knew he felt exactly the way she did.

She dropped one hand down from Deacon's shoulders and his fingers slipped in between hers perfectly, the whole motion smooth and seamless. His hand was warm and wrapped its heat around Jen's cool palm, pulsating rapidly in rhythm with her frantic heartbeat.

Unable to wait any longer, drawn to him like nothing she had ever felt before, Jen reached up towards Deacon, and he dipped his head down towards hers.

Their lips met, and it was as though Jen's entire life had been leading up to that moment, and the butterflies that had not left her all night swarmed through to her chest and drove her heart into a hysterical, pounding drumbeat.

She squeezed his hand tightly as he kissed her slowly, passionately. His free hand found the back of her neck and pulled her towards him with a powerful yearning. His lips were warm against hers and he breathed life into her in a way that didn't even seem possible.

Their eyes were closed, and so they did not see the sun finally disappear over the horizon, leaving only streaking traces behind it.

But they had not needed to see it, for what they had in that moment was worth a hundred and more sunrises and sunsets, and neither one of them dared let it go.

By the time the balloon descended, and the huge wicker basket eventually touched back down to the ground, all traces of the sun were gone, leaving behind the moon shining brighter and more luminescent than Jen had ever seen it. A thousand and more stars were dotted randomly across the sky, gazing down upon them with curious, sparkling eyes.

"And there you have it!" Deacon's inaptly named friend Grimm announced. "I do hope you've enjoyed yourselves!"

Jen smiled and blushed, though most certainly not for the first time that evening.

"We did, thank you Grimm." Deacon replied kindly, taking his friend's hand in a firm handshake. "Very much so."

Jen did notice, however, that Deacon kept one hand inescapably in hers the whole time.

"And might I say…" The strange and eccentric Walter Grimmway continued. "That you do indeed make the loveliest couple!"

Deacon laughed and put his arm back around Jen.

"Why, thank you." He thanked his odd and bizarrely likeable friend.

"Yes…" Jen added, extending her appreciative gaze out towards Grimm, though her words were a little tentative. "Thank you…"

"Aww shucks!" He replied jokingly, pretending to get embarrassed. "You two had better scoot before you make me blush!"

"Thanks again Grimm." Deacon bade him a fond farewell.

"Get outta here!" Grimm replied, laughing maniacally. "I'll see you soon!"

"That you will." Deacon replied and, doing as they were bid, he led Jen back to the car and held the door open for her once again.

"Let me take you home…" He offered formally, grinning the whole while.

Before Jen knew it, they were hurtling down pitch black, country lanes, and heading back towards Keepers Cottage.

She could still taste his lips on hers and she breathed slowly, trying to quiet her racing heart as she thought over and over again of their first kiss, high up in the sky under the golden rays of sunset, engrossed in her thoughts.

"Ready?" Deacon's voice broke her daydreaming then, and Jen looked around, blinking as if just waking from the deepest of slumbers.

They were back.

"Oh!" She exclaimed. "I didn't realise…"

Deacon smiled and slid his hand back into hers where it belonged, though he didn't speak.

His expression did all the talking.

"When will I see you again?" Jen asked all of a sudden, feeling a pit open up inside of her, filling her almost instantly with dread.

"Well…" He started, smiling his cheeky smirk and easing her worry. "I'm free right now…"

Jen blushed again, but then had an idea and glanced briefly up towards the house.

"Come with me." She suddenly replied. "I want to show you something."

There was not a moment's hesitation from Deacon.

"Of course. After you."

"Jen!?" Dyra called when she heard the front door open. She'd been wondering where her youngest daughter had been. "Jen!? Is that you!? I thought you finished earlier tod…"

But her mother didn't quite have chance finish her sentence, as Jen appeared around the corner to the kitchen with a particularly handsome young man in tow.

"Hi mom." Jen said immediately, and with not a single trace of hesitance. "This is Deacon."

"Oh! My…" Dyra tried to find her words, startled possibly more than she should have been.

"Pleasure." Deacon greeted her, extending his hand in his very formal, and at the same time, very casual manner of doing most things.

"Well...I..." Jen's mother attempted, in exactly the same way that her daughter sometimes stuttered, which made Deacon smile somewhat. "Please, call me Dyra." She eventually managed, taking his hand gratefully.

"Thank you, Dyra." Deacon replied, his rough velvety voice echoing through the house in a manner that neither Dyra nor her youngest daughter were used to.

"Well..." Jen's mother started then, picking up the last of the glasses she had been drying and placing them back in the cupboard above the worktop on the far wall, adjacent to the oven.

She opened the cupboard door only slightly, and closed it very quickly, as if she wanted to hide what might be inside.

Her concern over the matter was virtually unnoticeable, but Deacon saw it.

"Have you had a good evening?" She asked.

Deacon's gaze swept over the kitchen in an instant and fixed almost immediately on a framed picture of Dyra, Jen, and a third girl, whom he could only presume was Clare.

The three of them were standing in front of a lake. It looked to be a summer's day, and they seemed very happy. Deacon didn't know exactly where the picture had been taken, but judging by the fact that Dyra and Jen barely looked any different, it couldn't have been all that long ago.

"It was amazing, mom..." Jen began, her tone excited, not having noticed that Deacon had honed in so quickly on the picture he now held in his hand.

"We went up in a hot air balloon and the sun was setting and we…"

Of course Deacon knew what Jen had intended to say next, and smiled as she caught her tongue, almost forgetting who she was talking to.

"And what, sweetheart?" Dyra asked, though her gaze had fallen nervously upon the picture Deacon was holding.

"Is this Clare?" Deacon asked suddenly. Fortunately, and quite purposefully, cutting off potential embarrassment for Jen, but in turn, unfortunately, sending a wave of anxiety coursing through Dyra's veins.

"Yeah…" Jen replied, stepping round to Deacon's side and peering over his shoulder at the photo. "That was when we went to the lake…" She recalled, glancing briefly up at her mother.

"Is Clare here?" Deacon asked, glancing round for some reason, as if that would magically make her appear.

"No, I think she's out…" Jen replied carefully, stealing a quick look over at Dyra. "But she was at the beach earlier, and at The Rusty Oak…"

"Really?" Deacon queried, with genuine surprise in his voice.

How had he not seen her?

Even though she looked very similar to Jen, he didn't recognise the girl in this photo at all…

"Mom, I'm going to show Deacon sea view side." Jen changed the subject abruptly then, though Dyra looked no less concerned.

"You know I don't like you going up there…" Her mother said, concern in her tone still.

"We won't be long…" Jen replied by way of an argument, taking Deacon's hand and heading immediately for the stairs.

"Sea view side?" He queried.

"Just be careful please!" Dyra warned, cutting Jen off even before she could speak.

"We'll be fine, mom." Jen announced then. "Come on!" She ushered to Deacon as she practically dragged him up the stairs.

"Where are we going?" He questioned again.

"You'll see! I'll show you!"

Jen giggled and practically revelled in the chance to surprise him now, after the evening he'd given her.

Without hesitation, when she reached her bedroom, with Deacon still in tow, Jen made immediately for the window in the slanted ceiling.

"Grab that Walkman please." She asked him, pointing to the CD player lying on her ruffled bed, next to her black, felt CD case and pushing the window up and open easily with her other hand.

Her strength certainly seemed to be returning, along with her figure, Deacon noted, quite admirably.

"And the case…" Jen added on a whim, as she jumped up and pushed herself up out onto the roof, all in one smooth movement. "Pass them up here…"

Deacon handed Jen the Walkman and black, felt case, and she disappeared from view. He practically leapt up and out of the window, landing beside Jen on the rooftop, and she smiled at him thankfully.

"Come on…" She breathed, taking Deacon's hand and leading him up and over the apex of the roof.

The sky was still brilliantly clear, and above them an entire galaxy of stars swam amidst the blackness, hovering on the very edge of perpetual nothingness, with a dreadfully long way down on either side.

Glowing moonlight illuminated the breaking waves in the pitch black waters of the night, and the sight of it was mesmerising to watch.

"How often do you come up here?" Deacon asked quietly, though there didn't really seem to be any need for him to whisper.

He crouched low and sat beside Jen on the slanted roof, facing the coast.

"Clare and I come up every night…" She replied just as quietly, placing her Walkman in her lap and unzipping the black, felt case slowly.

"The two of you sound very close." Deacon commented, and though she could not see it, Jen knew he wore his cheeky, understanding smile in the dark of the night.

"We always have been…" She replied, though there was a haunting tone to her voice that Deacon couldn't quite place.

It was almost as if there was more that Jen wanted, or needed, to say. But, for some reason, she couldn't bring herself to speak of it.

Without another word, barely even able to see the CD's in the case because of the dim light, Jen began to flick through the pages by starlight.

She had done this practically every night now for almost as long as she could remember, and she knew very nearly the exact order of the CD's anyway as she thumbed through.

"What about that one?" Deacon asked suddenly, resting his hand upon the page Jen had just flicked over to, and she knew exactly which disc he meant.

From Clare xx

A silent, moral battle ensued within Jen then. But, strangely enough, she didn't come to the immediate conclusion that she thought she would.

In fact, it was the second time she had cast aside her concerns and come to this particular answer of late.

Screw it.

This taking chances thing was starting to become a habit…

Though, she imagined, it would only be a matter of time before her luck ran out…

She reached inside the wallet of the page and slipped the disc out and immediately into the Walkman, with a practiced finesse that she had perfected over many months.

Plugging in the headphones, Jen gave one earpiece to Deacon, put the other in her right ear, and leant her head almost instantly upon his shoulder. His arm came round to warm her and to keep her safe, and she had missed that feeling so much, for it was something that her older sister Clare never did any more.

The songs on the CD were old, cheesy, and in many cases, hilarious. It was safe to say that, for the first time in a long time, once more, Jen had a laugh and a joke with Deacon in a way that she had thought would never again be possible.

She was back on top of the world, for the second time that day.

After a while, partway through the disc, the moon and the stars had shifted enough, and their eyes had grown accustomed to the darkness so, that they could pretty much see everything they were doing.

Deacon produced from somewhere, Jen didn't quite know where, a pad and pencil, and he began sketching something across two thick pages. His hands moved so fast in the dim light that they were a blur, and pouring from his fingertips came the exquisite image of the two of them sat alone on the rooftop.

In the distance he drew the glowing horizon and the waves breaking on the shore, the stars and the moon, and somehow even the sky; though it was just blackness to look at, he brought it to life right in front of Jen's eyes.

As she watched him work she leant further and further into his chest, and his heavy heartbeat thudded a steady, calming rhythm in her ears, which, after only a little while longer, sent her cascading into yet another dream filled night.

This time though, whilst she might have felt safer than she had done in a very long time, Jen's mind and thoughts were still lost and troubled. They plagued her terribly as the hours of darkness wore on, and the cold seeped its way into every crevice.

The Façade

Young, troubled Jennifer Williams found herself in the same place in her dream that night as she had done previously. However, this time, she felt something looming ominously and precariously over her, taunting her as if she was supposed to know what it was.

The streetlights still lit evenly spaced yellow spotlights as far up and down Memoria Lane as she could see, though the road was more chokingly narrow than she had ever remembered it.

Shrubbery on either side of the lane pressed in closer than ever before, strangling the road and anybody who happened to pass along it, which, in this case, was only poor Jen.

Within moments of recognising once again where she was, Jen found her legs churning slowly, carrying her down the endless lane towards a destination unknown. In the back of her mind she knew, at some point or another in the past, her destination would have been the shop where Clare worked, or at least partway there to meet her.

All of a sudden, a hauntingly familiar but still startling noise, off to the side of the road, in the bushes, caught Jen off guard and she jumped in fright.

"Help!" She called immediately, and not for the first time. "Is anybody there!?"

But, as she knew would be the case, nobody came to her aid.

She tried to run again, but she couldn't move.

She tried to think of a way out of this, but her mind would not work.

The figure approached from the bushes once more, seeming to surgically separate itself from the shadows and glide over the ground towards her, its movements smooth and purposeful.

Horror gripped her.

But then, unexpectedly, fresh life flooded through her. It was a feeling she was becoming gratefully accustomed to, and she smiled with heavy relief when she saw that the figure was indeed again Deacon.

He didn't speak at first, and still she couldn't.

His hand swept up to the back of her neck and head, and he ran his fingers gently through her hair. Pulling her closer, kissing her lightly on her forehead, his touch filled Jen with warmth and security.

"Are you okay?" He asked her quietly, pulling her head into his chest so that she could feel his pulsating heartbeat yet again.

Jen couldn't speak, but instead she crept her hands up to clutch his shirt and nodded into him.

"What happened?" He asked her, his voice the softest and harshest of whispers.

"I…I don't…I don't kn…" Jen began, but even as she began to speak, she knew her words was false.

How could she keep living this lie?

"I…I can't…" She tried again, but the words, even though they were much closer to the truth, stuck in her throat like needles, lodging themselves in her windpipe, suffocating her with guilt.

Suddenly another noise from the bushes drew both their attentions, and Deacon looked over sharply, scanning everything with his all-seeing gaze.

"Why can't I see…?" He murmured, thinking aloud, frowning and looking again into the darkness.

But then Jen looked slowly up from where she had buried herself in his chest, shaking visibly.

"I can…" She whispered terribly.

Without another word she pulled her phone from her pocket, yet again in another well practiced movement, and turned on the torch.

The brilliant white light blinded them both for a second, but it illuminated the trees and the shrubs and the bushes for all to see.

In an instant the noise sounded again, and yet another figure rose up from the undergrowth, exploding into view, caught in the spotlight.

Whoever he was, he didn't say a word, and before either of them could get a good look at him, he took off between the trees, darting this way and that so as not to be seen.

"Who was that…?" Deacon asked Jen, knowing that somehow she held the answer to his question.

But she shook her head as she replied.

"He's not why we're here…" She replied knowingly, though her words didn't feel like her own.

Deacon looked at her with slightly wide eyes, but Jen's gaze remained focused intently on the treeline stretched out before them.

"So, why are we here…?" He whispered, naturally, for it was perhaps the most logical question to ask following such a statement.

Jen only sighed, and her whole body seemed to deflate with that single motion.

"Come on…" She whispered, taking slow, cautious, terrified steps forward, knowing that she had no choice in the matter.

This had already been decided.

She couldn't escape it now.

"What are we looking for…?" Deacon asked, pressing her still, as they approached the bushes and scanned the light through the undergrowth.

Jen sighed again.

"I try not to think about it…" She admitted, and very honestly so, all things considered.

Deacon opened his mouth to speak again, naturally wanting to ask why, but something stopped him. He realised all of a sudden that this, whatever it was, was very personal, and had plagued Jen for a very long time.

He decided not to push too far.

Within barely moments they found themselves peering between and through and over the bushes, getting closer and closer to the truth by the second.

Finally then, when they were upon what Deacon somehow knew they were here to find, they peered over a particularly thick bush, only to see on the other side the ground, very far away, and tinted orange by glorious sunset.

All of a sudden they found themselves stood together once more in the wicker basket, high up above the ground, peering carefully over the edge, drifting lazily in the evening breeze.

The blue and red balloon above them roared and flurried with hot air from the burner, and Grimm contentedly fired seemingly random jets of hot air up every now and then, keeping their altitude perfectly.

"What…?" Deacon looked around, bewildered. But when he glanced back to Jen, and saw her expression: happy, free of all worry and concern and fear and guilt, he knew all of a sudden exactly what her mind was doing.

This was a disguise.

A cover up.

A façade.

Jen's subconscious was shielding her from the truth. It was protecting her from whatever it was she had been holding on to so closely.

But at that point, even as Deacon's liquid eyes revealed all that he was coming to realise, it didn't really matter.

Their hands locked together, and then so did their lips. Brushing close and warm and full of hot, longing breath.

Jen had come very close to admitting the truth to herself, but now that Deacon had her, she had not come close enough.

It would seem that she still had a very long way to go.

Dyra's Warning

At some point or another during the long night, Jen and Deacon had made their way back down from the rooftop and into Jen's bed. Or perhaps, more accurately, onto Jen's bed, for when Jen awoke she found herself cradled in Deacon's arms, still fully clothed, and not even under the duvet.

It didn't matter.

She wasn't cold, and she was very comfortable, resting her head upon his shoulder and clutching his torso with her arms wrapped round him.

"Good morning." He greeted her warmly, his voice liquid and soft, and Jen smiled contentedly.

"Good morning." She replied.

"What were you dreaming about?" He asked, glancing down at her, and Jen looked back up at Deacon through slightly foggy eyes.

She should have known really.

Just as she could have guessed that he would, he had perceived she had been dreaming, and even more than that, that her dream had been significant.

"I don't know…" Jen half lied, unable to help herself. "We were looking for something, but we didn't find it, and we ended up back in the hot air balloon…"

She smirked at the mention of the Duchess, and Deacon's cheeky smile in return sent butterflies fleeting through Jen's body once more.

The sound of pots and pans knocking together echoed up the stairs then, distant and hollow.

"Mom's awake…" Jen noted, though her tone was indecipherable.

"We should go and say good morning…" Deacon commented, and Jen grinned in return.

"You can…" She joked seriously. "I'm going to have a shower…"

Though she might have changed after work yesterday, before their date, still all Jen could smell were the scents of the kitchen on her clothes and in her hair.

Realising in an instant that she was deadly serious, Deacon grinned in return and raised his eyebrows, rolling his eyes jokingly.

"You're impossible."

Jen laughed and kissed him softly as if things had always been this way, running her hands through his hair with fingers that ached for more.

"Good morning Deacon." Dyra greeted him as he descended the stairs and entered the kitchen to find her prepping for breakfast, pulling pots and pans and plates from cupboards and drawers left, right and centre.

"Good morning Dyra." He replied cheerfully. "How are you?"

"Very well thank you." She responded with a chuckle. "Actually…" She continued, pausing in her preparations to look him dead in the eye, somewhat disconcertingly, he had to confess. "Better than I've been in a long while…"

"Really…?" He asked, surprise evident in his tone. "Why's that?"

"I haven't seen Jennifer this happy for far too long…" Dyra explained, though her justification left more questions in Deacon's churning mind than it did answers.

"I see…" Deacon commented, not really knowing what else to say, for some reason once again picking up the picture he had examined the night previous, of the three of them stood by the lake. "Well…" He continued. "You should be proud. You have two very beautiful girls here…"

He looked up at Dyra then from the photo, and her eyes were a complete mystery to him, which even in of itself was something most unusual.

There were pictures everywhere of Jen and Clare, and of the three of them, Jen, Clare and Dyra.

Nowhere to be found, however, was there any kind of father figure.

Dyra looked as though she wanted to reply, but just couldn't bring herself to speak the words forming in her mind.

Eventually she managed to find her tongue, but Deacon knew in an instant that her words were not the real truth she wished to speak.

"Please look after Jen…" She managed. "Please be understanding. She doesn't mean it…"

Of course, the all too obvious question came immediately to the tip of Deacon's tongue, but for some reason he refrained from asking it.

He was usually so perceptive, but alas, here he found himself, with absolutely no idea what Dyra meant.

There were so many things that seemed to be eluding him of late.

Albatross

He felt as though there was something going on here, some secret, so locked away and deep rooted, that he was simply out of his depth with it all.

"I will…" He promised, naturally.

What else could he say?

He had no idea.

Nonetheless, amidst everything, he couldn't help but feel as though Dyra's cautionary words sounded almost like a warning. As if there was something he needed to prepare for.

"Jen really seems to be doing much better…" Dyra continued, pressing on regardless of the clear confusion painted across Deacon's face, though now her eyes had turned back to the pots and pans and cupboards and cutlery. "She looks much better too. She's a stunning girl, but she hasn't been looking after herself…"

"Doing much better…?" Deacon questioned. "Not looking after herself…?" He pressed. "Why? What's happened…?"

Suddenly it was as if Dyra realised that she'd said too much, and she cut off almost immediately. Her words that followed, Deacon could sense, weren't the whole truth, or anywhere near it in fact.

"Well…" She started, her tone wavering. "Things haven't been the same since her father left, and, well, you know…" Dyra quickly trailed off.

As a matter of fact, Deacon did know, for his family life growing up hadn't always consisted of roses and rainbows, but then, he knew that wasn't really the problem here.

But he had nothing else to go on.

"My family haven't always been the easiest either…" He agreed, nodding his head and pursing his lips, doubting her words silently, and only in his mind. "I guess these things just happen…" He posed, pushing the matter slightly, wanting the full truth now, but knowing he wasn't going to get it. "We don't always get a choice, do we?"

"No…" Dyra agreed, sighing with deep concern.

She looked up briefly and caught Deacon's gaze, knowing that he could see she was hiding something.

"Maybe someday Jennifer will tell you herself…" Dyra commented then, as if she was thinking out loud, and by way of confirming that she was lying. At the same time though, she sealed the fact that she would reveal no more.

"Perhaps…" Deacon agreed, though what he had just agreed to, he wasn't entirely sure.

There came the sound of footsteps from upstairs and Jen began to make her way down to the kitchen.

Dyra had finished getting everything out, but it seemed that she was going to leave the actual cooking to Jen.

"I'm a terrible cook." She explained to Deacon, laughing slightly, trying to ease the tension she had created. "Jen loves to cook. And she's so much better at it than I am…"

"Can I get you a drink?" Deacon offered, glancing over to the kettle.

"Why, thank you, Deacon." Dyra replied, and he moved immediately to the cupboard adjacent to the oven, where he had seen Dyra replace her glass the previous night.

"Wait! Deacon…" She urged quickly, just as he began to open the cupboard door.

"Yes…?" He asked, pausing, and her expression was fraught.

"The mugs are in the one below…" She answered, her tone wavering once more, trying to hide her concern.

"Ah!" He replied, leaning down and retrieving three crock mugs from the cupboard at his feet.

However, though he'd cracked open the cupboard door only ever so slightly, Deacon had seen, of course, what Dyra hadn't wanted him to.

He pretended to ignore the fact, as if he hadn't seen anything, and tried to push the image of bottles upon bottles and boxes upon boxes of prescription medications, all lined up along the top shelf of the cupboard, far away and out of his mind.

Had Dyra known how perceptive Deacon was, she would have been perhaps a little more concerned. But for now, at least, everything continued as it should have done, apart from the reams of questions building up uncontrollably in Deacon's mind.

He was desperately trying to fit together the pieces of this bizarre jigsaw, but every time he thought he was coming close, a hundred more fragments were thrown at him, leaving him feeling lost all over again.

"Morning!" Jen greeted her mother as she frolicked into the kitchen, setting her hands immediately to work on breakfast, without even the slightest hesitation.

Her hair was still wet and tied up into a bun to keep it out of the way.

"Good morning, Jennifer." Dyra replied, clutching the cup of coffee Deacon had just handed her.

Within minutes Deacon and Jen were waltzing round the kitchen, singing and dancing with and between each other, and somehow, amidst the whole spectacle, cooking eggs, bacon, sausages, tomatoes, and anything else they could lay their hands on for breakfast.

Jen's voice soared, just as it had always used to, and Deacon's wasn't half bad either, Dyra noted.

"So, what are you two doing today?" Jen's mother eventually asked, once the food was all ready and they sat down to eat.

Jen looked expectantly at Deacon, and he gathered by her expression that she wasn't working.

"Well, I have to nip home…" He started between mouthfuls. "I have a few things I need to get done…" Then he looked over at Jen. "If you'd like to come?" He asked.

Jen nodded and smiled, her mouth full of bacon and egg.

"Have you spoken to Clare?" Dyra asked then, her question and her gaze very direct, looking intently at her youngest daughter.

Jen swallowed nervously.

"Not so much over the past few days…" Jen admitted.

"Good." Dyra replied, with something in her voice that wasn't quite venom, but that wasn't overly pleasant either.

Deacon, of course, didn't comment, but silently he was shocked.

What on Earth…?

"Do you live far, Deacon?" Dyra asked then, cutting that particular conversation off and turning her gaze upon him again, and for not the first time that morning.

Her expression was strange, and entirely unreadable.

Something wasn't right here.

Deacon could feel it.

"I've moved quite a few times…" He started apprehensively.

"I know that feeling…" Jen agreed, and for some reason knowing that Deacon was a bit of a drifter too made Jen feel slightly better about the whole thing, though Dyra didn't say a word on the matter.

"I live about twenty minutes down the coast…" He told them.

"Do you live with family?" Jen asked then, for some reason feeling the sudden, fleeting urge to meet them.

But a flash of regret crossed Deacon's face at her words, and instantly Jen wished she could take back her question.

"No…" He replied carefully, his gaze darting between Jen's stricken face and her mother's stony expression. "I don't…"

HOME

It was perhaps half an hour or so later that Jen found herself once again in Deacon's car, hurtling down the coastline towards his home. She didn't know exactly where they were going, but she trusted him; perhaps more so than she trusted most people.

And, unfortunately, that included her own mother, Dyra. Particularly after a few things she'd said, and the way she'd acted that morning.

Deacon had been quiet since they'd left, and looked deep in thought, and Jen didn't want to breach the silence just yet.

She could only imagine what her mother had told him while she'd been upstairs.

How could she have been so stupid as to let Dyra get him alone!?

Whatever she'd told him, though Jen doubted it was the full truth, it couldn't have been good…

Deacon reached out suddenly and flicked from the radio and over to his Bluetooth, selecting a band that Jen had never heard before, as they shot into a mountainside through a lengthy tunnel, under the orangey glow of artificial lights.

When they emerged back out into the sunshine, Jen cast her gaze out to her left and at the steep drop off from the side of the road, leading directly down to the water below.

The ocean swelled and rose dramatically and glistened green and blue and turquoise all at once. In the far distance offshore, wind turbines spun erratically in the howling winds. Jen watched them turn in frantic rhythm, as the band she did not know sung about cinnamon and lipstick and summer and love and living and believing.

On the whole, she had to admit, she quite liked them.

They passed through yet another two tunnels, and the road grew very narrow and wound its way left and right precariously between high sided cliffs on one side, and steep drop offs on the other.

Deacon's driving was impeccable however, and Jen felt not even in the least bit uneasy.

Soon enough he left the main road and turned down another lane, picking up speed between bends and flying round corners smoothly.

Another song by the same band came on then.

'You might have got the best of me, but you'll never get the rest of me…'

How apt, Jen thought to herself, considering the circumstances.

No one had got the best of her yet, except perhaps Clare.

Did she even have anything left to give?

Or had she already lost most of what made her, well, her?

Almost before she knew it they had arrived, and Deacon pulled into the drive of a house that looked like something of a holiday home.

Large, front facing doors and windows revealed tall, white walls, lined with balconies and spiral staircases visible through the expanses of glass. The driveway extended a full two dozen feet out from the front door, framed on either side by lush grass and flowers.

There was a single step that led up to the door, and looked like it was made entirely from white marble.

Deacon immediately stepped out and Jen followed him inside, as he unlocked the large, glass paned front door and remotely turned on the lights.

She was in awe.

"This is incredible…" Jen breathed almost immediately.

The house was spotless. The walls were for the most part white, with only limited decoration, and most of the surfaces were clear of anything at all.

"Thank you." Deacon replied, tilting his head slightly in acknowledgement. "I've moved around so much that I've never really seen the point in settling anywhere…" He admitted then, delving into a cupboard in the kitchen, open plan with the rest of downstairs, and pulling a glass from a shelf. "But I do like it here…" He confessed.

Pouring Jen a drink, he set the glass down for her on one of the worktops.

"Thanks." She said, smiling.

"Make yourself at home." He offered then, spreading his arms and glancing around. "I'm just going to change."

Jen nodded, and in moments she was alone in this marvellous house, and immediately her eyes tried to be everywhere at once, not knowing what to examine first.

She settled, perhaps quite predictably, upon a plaque that decorated one of the whitewashed walls in the vast living room, sparsely populated with furniture, barely enough even to make it look liveable.

Award for Artistic Excellence

Presented to Mr Deacon Ash

That took Jen aback somewhat.
But then, as her eyes traced around the wall and fell upon a painting that she had at first thought was simply decoration, she grasped all of a sudden the seeming extent of Deacon's talent.
Indeed, the exquisite piece that she now set her eyes upon was for decoration, but as she looked at the signature in the bottom right hand corner, it was only then that she realised it was Deacon's work.
Jen's breath caught in her throat, for two reasons.
The first, because somehow, impossibly, the painting was of an albatross.
The majestic bird soared over the ocean, looking down upon a person stranded on a desert island, surrounded by only a few sparse trees. The person had etched into the damp sand a message: a single word.
But whilst you might have expected SOS, or HELP, this was not the case.
Instead, the single word that this person had spelled out sent something of a chilling shiver racing up and down Jen's spine.

Ross Turner

HOME

And then the second reason, though by no means any less dramatic, was the brass plate that accompanied the piece.

By Mr Deacon Ash

Original sold for £250,000.00

That was, just, insane.
Jen continued to wander in astonishment.
Besides those pictures and plaques she had already seen, there was nothing else hung on any of the walls downstairs.
There were no family photos, no portraits, nothing.
The furniture, though sparse, was modern and artistic in of its own right. Small leather settees floated in the large, open plan living room. Tables and chairs were placed deceptively here and there, as if one might at any time decide to stop and sit and draw.
However, what Jen hadn't initially noticed, upon those tables and worktops, were piles of drawings, sketches and doodles, some half-finished and some barely started, dotted all over the place.
They were parts of people, animals, places, coastlines, horizons over vast wastelands, skylines over great endless cities, each and every one so realistic and lifelike that she half expected them to come to life right before her very eyes.

She headed back over towards the kitchen, and again her gaze swept over the room, noticing things she had not seen before.

Where at first she had seen clear table tops, though she didn't know why, now she saw that there were pens and pencils strewn about here and there, scattered across the top of yet another half-finished drawing.

This one was much bigger than the others, covering a full half of an A3 sheet of paper.

Pushing the pencils over to one side, yet again, what Jen saw stole her breath away.

It was the partly finished portrait of a girl. Catching it in one light, the picture looked so much like her that it may as well have been a photograph. But then, as she caught it in another light, the drawing was the spitting image of Clare; the resemblance was uncanny, and in fact quite spooky.

"Do you like it?" Deacon's voice suddenly sounded from the doorway, and Jen practically jumped out of her skin in fright.

"OH! Oh my God Deacon!" She gasped, leaning forwards onto her knees, her heart thumping heavily.

"I'm sorry!" He apologised immediately, rushing to her side, though he struggled to contain a laugh. "I didn't mean to startle you."

"It's okay..." She wheezed, chuckling slightly. "You were just so quiet. You scared the life out of me!"

"Are you okay?" He asked, his voice low and quite serious, as he placed one hand on Jen's arm.

"I'm fine." Jen assured him. "Just don't do that every time you come downstairs please!" She joked.

"I only came down and walked in!" He responded, feigning shock.

"Yeah! Like a bloody ninja!" Jen poked back at him.

They both fell about laughing, and then Jen turned her attention again to the half-finished portrait.

"So, who's this supposed to be?" She asked him, wearing a smirk as she spoke.

"Who does it look like?" He bartered.

"It looks like me." Jen replied quite simply.

"It is you."

"Just me?"

Jen's question was a simple one, but Deacon paused for a moment. There seemed to be a much deeper meaning to what she was asking him.

"If you want it to be…" He replied curiously, grinning cheekily as he spoke, making Jen blush slightly. "It can be just you, if you let it…"

That particular comment didn't really make too much sense to Jen, and so she just let it pass, and her eyes wandered to the all but vacant walls of Deacon's home once more.

"Deacon…" Jen started, stepping closer to him and resting her head upon his chest, leaning her body close to his as he wrapped his arms around her.

"Yes, Jen?" He responded automatically, though somehow he already knew what her question would be.

"You don't see much of your family, do you?" She asked, and again he knew that wasn't the only question she was posing.

"No…I don't…" He started in return.

Jen felt a knot forming in her stomach.

"Don't you see them at all?" She pressed, admittedly a little shocked, reading between the lines.

Deacon smiled ruefully.

It seemed he wasn't the only perceptive one here.

The answer to her question was painfully obvious by Deacon's silence, and Jen bit her lip cautiously.

"It must be hard…" She continued then, her voice thick with emotion. "To know they're out there, and never to see them?" Jen pressed on relentlessly. "What if one day you knew you'd never have the chance to see them again? Would you regret it?"

Deacon pulled back, looking at Jen very directly. His hair was still wet from his shower and for some reason she felt the sudden urge to run her hands through it.

"Family can mean a lot of different things…" He told her, his voice level and his tone sombre, as if he'd had this thought many times. "It doesn't have to be blood. It can be whatever we make of it." His words were quiet and full of emotion, thick with sadness, yet also resolve.

Neither of them spoke then, and they simply held each other's gaze a moment longer, and then a moment more.

Deacon's fingers found their way into Jen's hair and he kissed her, his lips warm against hers, pulling her in closely and tightly, in the way that every young girl wishes.

Her hands did indeed find their way into his hair too, and Deacon's slid down Jen's back, sending shivers running up and down her spine.

His tongue found hers and Jen felt herself drawn into him like never before. It was a desperate, longing feeling that she couldn't control, and it overtook her body like a wild animal, fuelling her with crazed desire and hunger.

She found her hands exploring his body and her fingers traced gently up and down his chest, while his continued to send goose bumps racing over her exposed arms and shoulders. Jen shivered every time with sheer delight as it pulsed through her, making her short of breath, and only driving her to pull Deacon evermore fanatically closer.

Then, before she even knew what she was doing, Jen felt her hands delving beneath his shirt and running up his stomach and chest, hungrily exploring everywhere they could reach. His body was smooth, coarse, soft, rough, all at once; well defined and perfectly crafted, it made Jen's heart race and sent a hungry, forbidden fire racing through her veins.

But, amidst her insatiable wanderings, Jen's hands traced up and over Deacon's chest once again, heaving beneath her aching palms, and her fingers found something that caused her roaming to cease.

Something on his chest.
Up towards his collarbone.
On his ribs.

They were flat and smooth, smoother than the rest of his skin, and had rough, harsh edges, at least a couple of inches across.

In her moment of hesitation, Jen's other hand paused too, further round the side of Deacon's chest.

Another one.

The same shape.

The same size.

Jen pulled away slowly, though not once did she break Deacon's grasp, nor his gaze. It was a look he gave her that made her wonder endlessly what she should do.

Breathing heavily, looking up through concerned eyes, thick with emotion, her expression spoke a thousand and more words that she need not utter.

His eyes looked deeply troubled as he gazed back down at her, though there was adoration there as well, all too clearly.

Suddenly then, though she didn't know exactly how, Jen understood, and when she spoke, her words came out in a whisper so soft that the sound of them sent shivers of her own cascading up and down Deacon's spine.

Now it was she who had him.

"Show me…"

The Grotto

Deacon slowly rolled his top up from the bottom, and Jen pushed it up and over his head, her hands trembling as she did so, running her fingers and palms over his stomach and chest.

From what Jen could see and feel, from Deacon's hips up to his chest, his body was so well defined that it may as well have been sculpted. She was too caught up in the moment however, and besides, that wasn't the only thing she was focusing on.

In an instant Jen's hands found the scars on his chest and ribs that she had felt beneath his shirt, and she glanced down to see them. They were silvery and smooth and rough all at once, and she touched them delicately, a little afraid even.

The worst of them was the first one she'd found, two inches long, thin, though there were three in total across his broad chest.

The kinds of scars a blade would leave behind.

Jen ran her hands round to the sides of Deacon's ribs, and found yet even more scars than she'd discovered earlier, and she traced her fingers over them delicately, kissing his chest softly.

They were like puncture wounds, slipping between his ribs here and there.

But then, the most terrifying of all, came when Jen slid her hands gracefully round to run tenderly up and down Deacon's back. Her eyes widened and she swallowed nervously, though she did not speak, and continued to kiss his chest fondly, wishing she could heal his wounds and erase all memory of them completely.

Raising her hands up onto his shoulders, Jen slowly turned Deacon so that he was facing away from her, and he complied, allowing her to move him, turning slowly and dropping his arms to his sides as if in defeat.

His torso and shoulders were broad and strong, though his back tapered in at his waist, giving his body a lean, triangular shape.

When she saw his back however, her mouth agape slightly, Jen caressed it with her fingers as softly as she possibly could, not wanting to hurt him. Of course, she knew the scars didn't hurt now, but the pain they must have caused him in the past, she daren't even begin to imagine.

Lined across his back, taking Jen's breath away and bringing tears to her eyes, were literally hundreds of scars, long and straight and thin, each one at least half a foot in length. They all sat horizontally, or just slightly off, one by one on top of each other, all the way up and down his back, from the very tops of his shoulders, right down to his coccyx.

Deacon cringed and winced slightly and Jen ran her hands across them, tracing her fingers lightly up and down his spine. His shoulders lifted a little as he tensed reflexively, but after a few moments he began to relax, settling, and his shoulders dropped again.

Jen kissed him gently on his back, making her way up and across the arch of his shoulders.

Deacon leaned his head back and rested it gently against Jen's as she clutched him tightly, kissing the back of his neck and wishing he'd never had to suffer so.

Sometime later, Jen's hand was in Deacon's, as it seemed to be almost permanently now, and that was just the way she liked it.

The afternoon sun looked down pleasantly upon them as they walked, and bathed them in its warm tenderness.

Deacon had driven her most of the way back home, but they'd stopped off by the coast before they'd reached Keepers Cottage.

They weren't finished yet.

"I've never told anybody about this before…" Deacon admitted. "It was my dad mainly. Everybody else was scared of him, so they just did what he told them…"

Jen didn't speak.

She just listened, squeezing Deacon's hand tightly.

She knew this couldn't have been easy.

"I think my mom used to try to stand up to him, but he would beat her until she was unconscious, wait for her to wake up, and then beat her again. She stopped trying to fight him a long time ago…"

Deacon sighed heavily.

"It was hard times. We lived in a rough area." He continued. "My dad thought drawing and painting was soft. He said it was a waste of time and money.

He always said he would beat it out of me. Ever since I was little…"

He smiled ruefully then, defiance clear in his eyes.

"He hasn't managed it yet, but if I was still there, I know he'd still be trying. I had to get out. I had to get away…"

Jen nodded, though she was physically incapable of imagining what it must have been like.

It must have been awful.

"How…?" She managed to ask then, her voice a little shaky.

"With a belt, usually." Deacon replied casually, as if shrugging the whole thing off. "But with whatever he had to hand at the time really."

"What about the…?" Jen started. Faltering for a moment. "What about the others…?" She asked, and Deacon knew exactly what she meant.

The ones that looked like puncture wounds.

He nodded slowly, as if confirming her worst fears.

"They were from a knife…"

Jen's breath caught and she felt physically sick to her stomach.

"They weren't about the drawings though…" Deacon began to explain. "They were when he came home drunk one night. Don't get me wrong, he came home drunk most nights. But this time he was ruthless…"

Even Jen's breaths quivered as Deacon spoke, and she found that she was shaking slightly, petrified.

"He came back late. Really late. My mom said something. I don't know what, but it annoyed him. It really annoyed him. He went nuts."

Deacon spoke in short, sharp breaths; stating only fact.

As they walked, the coastline in view now, though upon a section of it that Jen did not know, Deacon's gaze was everywhere, and she knew that he saw everything, both in the past and in the present.

"He started to hit her." He continued. "Hard. I was getting older, and I'd had enough. It was stupid, but I was only protecting her. I threw myself in between them. I tried to fight him off."

Jen wanted to ask a hundred and more questions.

She wanted to hold him and make all the painful memories vanish.

But she couldn't.

She knew they would be with him forever.

And she understood that perhaps better than most.

"He came at me with a knife." Deacon continued, reminiscing the whole event as clear as day. "We were in the kitchen. It was only a small room. My mother was behind me. I had nowhere to go."

He laughed suddenly then, though remorsefully, and looked up at the huge expanse of sky swallowing everything below it, his voice thick with emotion.

"I was lucky. He did this one first." He said, tapping his chest where Jen knew the biggest of the scars was. "He forced the knife through my ribs and wrenched it left and right. He missed my heart though. He only punctured my lung. When I didn't die straight away, he lost it. He just started stabbing at me wildly, randomly, all over the place."

Jen knew exactly how many more times Deacon's father had got him. She had counted the scars herself, but she didn't interrupt.

"He got me twice more in the chest. Twice in the ribs that side…" He continued, indicating to the left of his torso. "And four times on that side…" He said then, pointing to his right side.

He laughed again, though it wasn't funny in the slightest.

He was simply dredging humour out of terror.

"Makes sense. He was a lefty…"

"I…I can't…I can't imagine…" Jen attempted, but her words were lost in her shock. "Did he…? Did they call someone? An ambulance? The police?"

"It was close." Deacon admitted. "Very close. I was rushed to hospital in an ambulance. I think the police were probably involved too. I don't really know. As soon as I was well enough, pretty much as soon as I could stand, I ran."

Jen reached round to Deacon's side and pulled him into her arms.

"It gave me a bit of a different perspective on life." He admitted, pulling Jen close, feeling her body against his.

"I like your perspective." Jen replied immediately.

And indeed she did.

It was different.

It was unique.
Everything happens for a reason.

Before long they found themselves on the beachfront, and after the revelations about Deacon's past, they both needed a moment to let it all soak in. And so they just walked, hand in hand still, the stones crunching beneath their feet, seagulls cawing all around, diving down upon unsuspecting tourists, harassing them and stealing as much food as possible.

There was no sign of the albatross, Jen noted. But also, and perhaps more unusually, there had been no sign of Clare either.

Perhaps they were both preoccupied with other things?

That was an interesting thought, but Jen's mind didn't allow her to grasp exactly why, and so she skimmed over the notion without realising quite what she was missing.

"Come on!" Deacon suddenly exclaimed, pulling Jen by the hand as he surged forwards, cutting down onto the sandy portion of the beach.

"Where are we going!?" Jen laughed.

He turned midstride and winked at her slyly.

"I know a good place…" He replied mysteriously.

Deacon led Jen down across the sand, right next to where the surf frothed and seethed, and then up again onto the rocks on the far side on the beach. Following what looked at first glance to be an impossible route, Deacon forged round the very furthest corner of the rocky coastline that Jen had spent so many months simply gazing at.

They skipped from rock to rock, gaining speed and momentum, hurtling faster and faster. He was quick, but then so was she, and she just about managed to keep pace with him as they flung themselves over treacherous crevasses and monstrous drops.

The rock ledges dropped off suddenly then, their faces sheer and vertical; impossible to traverse, descending all the way down to the water.

"Where now?" Jen asked, breathing heavily, her lungs heaving, excited.

The salty wind whipped at her long, curly hair, and the sun kissed her face warmly as it shone down upon the coastline.

"Here." Deacon pointed, holding out his hand towards a slight opening in the rock. The crack looked barely wide enough for even a child squeeze through, and Jen could see no more than two feet inside of it, for it was too dark and too narrow.

"In there?" She questioned, her tone dubious, and quite rightly so.

"Don't worry." He assured her confidently. "It opens up pretty much straight away once you're inside."

Sea spray rocketed up over the ledge upon which they stood, clearing at least two dozen feet from the water far below, as a wave struck the rocks perfectly, sending crashing water off in every direction.

"Do you trust me?" Deacon asked her, looking at Jen pointedly, and her reply was instant, and automatic.

"I do." She breathed, surprising even herself.

But she didn't have much time to think on it, as Deacon surged forward, letting go of her hand, and dropped down with practiced grace of his own into the crevasse in the rocks so narrow, and disappeared into the rock face itself.

"I'm here!" His voice called up to her from the blackness. "Don't worry!"

Surprisingly, Deacon's words spurred Jen on immediately, and also, just as astonishingly, the thought in the back of her mind that this was just the sort of thing Clare would do spurred her on too.

Jen dropped down into the dark, narrow crevasse, following the sound of Deacon's voice.

She did not see her albatross soar overhead as she descended, looking down upon her with satisfaction in his jet black gaze.

Her descent was not quite as graceful, nor practiced, as Deacon's, but it got the job done.

She couldn't tell where she was going at first, and she started to panic, reaching out desperately with one hand and struggling to find her footing. But in an instant he had her, gripping her hand tightly with his, and Jen calmed almost immediately.

Dropping her head beneath an enormous boulder, splaying both her hands on the walls, Jen glanced down, and indeed the narrow cave widened dramatically, just as Deacon had promised.

His legs were planted on either side of the cavern walls, about four or five feet lower than where Jen hovered, quite precariously to say the least.

"Okay?" He checked, and she nodded in response, concentrating on where she was putting her feet. He pointed this way and that to help her, and she placed her feet and hands exactly where he indicated, finding, in fact, that it was actually quite easy. She descended quickly, dropping down at Deacon's side in barely even a minute.

A huge archway stretched up and over the pair of them, as they lowered themselves the final few feet out of the cavern.

"This is the Grotto." Deacon stated, his gaze sweeping over the cavern stretching beyond the archway.

"The Grotto?" Jen queried.

"I'll show you." He promised, taking her hand gently and leading her under the massive archway, their footsteps echoing round the cavern and they traversed its side.

Clearly this cavern always flooded when the tide came it, and the walls were wet and slippery.

Jen followed Deacon still and they climbed up a little. There was still a fair amount of water in the bottom of the cave, and it looked almost crystal clear, which was most odd for the water round these parts, Jen thought.

Towards the back of the cavern the walls opened up and widened, giving way to a stretch of golden sand and a much larger pool of water that shone and glistened with sunlight.

At first Jen didn't see how that was possible, and looked puzzled at the sight, since they were too far back in the cave for the sunlight to reach here.

But then she saw what was happening, and all became clear.

The reason the pool was so deep, and the reason it shone and glistened so brightly, was because although they stood in a cave, beneath the surface of the water there was a break in the cavern wall, which led out to the open ocean, allowing the sunlight to filter through.

This was the Grotto.

Jen grinned mischievously.

Now she understood.

Unless you knew about the cave they had climbed through, fancied dropping down the sheer rock face, or knew about the secret Grotto that led here from the open water, there was simply no way to get here.

It was not the sort of place you could just stumble across. Not unless you were looking for it.

"I've been here a few times…" Deacon explained then, his rough velvety voice echoing round the cavern a hundred times. "But I've never shown it to anybody…"

"How did you find it?" Jen asked, mystified at the place, gazing all around.

It was something out of a fantasy.

The way the cave glistened from the underwater sunlight, so secret and so secluded. There was no way it could possibly be real.

"I stumbled across it." Deacon admitted. "I was looking for a secluded spot to draw. I had no idea I'd find this…"

"Well, I think you found a secluded spot alright!" Jen laughed, and her happiness echoed all about her. "Why are you showing me?" She asked, and Deacon looked across at her quite seriously.

"Are you ready?" He asked in return, his voice low.

Albatross

"For what?"
"To look for desert islands…"

Elusive Desert Islands

Jen was confused.

She frowned slightly.

Deacon grinned at her and stepped easily over the wet, slippery rocks of the Grotto, moving purposefully, though she knew not what he intended.

Desert islands?

Jen thought of the picture she had seen hung back at Deacon's house, though why that specifically jumped into her mind at that moment, she wasn't sure.

Recalling the albatross looking down upon the desert island, and the message etched into the sand, she wandered what on Earth Deacon meant.

But, in her wonderings, Jen had failed to notice that Deacon had dropped down from the rocks and onto the golden strip of sand that lined the pool in the bottom of the cavern: the one that led out into the open water.

When she looked up, distracted from her thoughts by the sound of echoing ripples disturbing the silence, she saw that he was walking slowly out into the lush water. The pool grew ever greener and ever bluer the further he waded out, and also, more notably, she saw that he'd left his clothes up on the rocks.

He turned back and smirked at her in perhaps the cheekiest manner Jen had seen yet, and she blushed red furiously. But it wasn't entirely his smile that made her flush so dramatically, she had to admit, as her eyes wandered in awe over his terribly perfect, terribly scarred body.

Jen felt as if her heart was about to leap from her chest, and her mouth hung slightly agape in sheer, undisguised awe.

He was flawless.

Her fingers ached to touch him.

Her bosom heaved and longed to be pressed against his chest.

Then, with the same smirk and a subtle wave of his hand, Deacon beckoned for Jen to follow him in.

Suddenly her stomach lurched.

How could she do that?

It was too much.

She couldn't.

Could she?

Jen's instant reaction was to raise her hands warily, shaking her head slightly and taking a small step back.

Deacon still wasn't very far out, and he wasn't fully facing her, but the water was so impossibly clear. It rose up to his hips, although, if Jen was perfectly honest, it hid pretty much nothing; not that she wished for it to be any other way.

But then, as if reading her thoughts, Deacon took another step further away from her and, in a single movement, dove head first beneath the water.

He knew what she needed.

He always knew.

And he knew he could get her to follow him in.

And follow him she would.

He surfaced from the water again, turning to face her now, and the crystal clear pool came up to his chest. The water glistened on his wet scars and his body looked somehow even more defined than it had done before, every detail highlighted by the glimmering of the Grotto.

Jen smiled and, deciding to risk everything, just because all of a sudden she could, she rolled her dress up from the bottom and slowly pulled it over the top of her head.

She felt suddenly free for the first time in a long time.

Raising her arms up high, she slipped the dress over her hands and dropped it onto the rocks beside Deacon's clothes, kicking off her shoes as she did so, and her heart started to race furiously.

As she stood there in her lingerie, exposed, her nerves kicked in again, only this time tenfold. But she refused to yield.

Deacon smiled and, seeming to know as always what she was thinking, he politely turned his back and dropped again beneath the water, diving much deeper this time, looking almost even as if he was going to pass beneath the Grotto and out into the open water of the ocean.

Heart in her mouth, or maybe more accurately out on her sleeve: so far so that it was ridiculous, and potentially very dangerous, Jen carefully slipped off what little remained of her clothes, dropping them with the rest, and sidled down to the water's edge.

When she stepped out into the pool, breaching its surface cautiously, it was so icy cold that it stole her breath away, and not for the first time that day.

Wading out to about thigh depth, Jen moved slowly, taking very deep breaths in a futile attempt to counter the freezing temperature.

But then Deacon suddenly resurfaced once more, yet again a little further out. He faced away from her still, and now he was paddling to stay afloat. He was directly above the tunnel which led out to the open water, and the floor was about two dozen feet below him.

On an instinct, Jen dove head first into the ice cold pool, aiming for the mouth of the Grotto.

In an instant, fully submerged for the first time, she felt revitalised.

The water was so cold and fresh that she suddenly felt more alive than she ever had done.

Surfacing at Deacon's side after a few moments, her hands finding his body immediately, this was perhaps the most exciting thing Jen had ever done, and she could feel by his touch that it was completely new to him too.

How she could tell that, she wasn't exactly sure, but it just felt right, and she was glad that they could share this together.

Firsts are important.

Deacon held Jen closely and kissed her gently, his tender lips fiery compared to the icy cold water. And she kissed him back, passion welling up from deep inside of her. It was something that he had sparked within Jen's very soul, and there was no quelling it.

Barely even three days ago had she felt it for the first time, and since then the feeling had built inside of her, growing and growing endlessly, until Jen felt as if her heart would burst.

 She didn't know what it was.

 Perhaps Clare had been right?

 Either way, she didn't really care.

 Whatever it was, she loved it.

 Deacon's strong arms came up and around Jen's back, pulling her body close against his as they floated. She felt his heart surging through the cold water towards her as they pressed together.

 Pulling her legs up through the water and wrapping them around Deacon's waist, she felt his heat flowing through her, rushing inside of her in a way she'd never imagined.

 He pressed himself somehow even closer to her, and Jen arched her back and dropped her head into the water, allowing it to engulf her completely, pulling herself ever further into him.

 She crossed her feet behind him, linking them together and pulling hard, and the sensation rippled through her body madly, intensely.

 His hands raked slowly and tenderly up and down her back and legs in the freezing water, and Jen gasped desperately to catch her breath as Deacon stole it away yet again.

Lost in You, Again

The moonlight cast the magic of its midnight glow across the ocean, as it did every night, dripping white, glimmering traces upon the ripping water's surface, leaving long trails in the wake of the midnight sun.

But tonight things were different.

The weather was closing in and the temperature had dropped dramatically. Clouds swarmed menacingly in the darkness and did their utmost to block the moonbeams at every opportunity.

Blustery winds whipped about and charged over the water and barraged exposed rock faces, whipping the waves into furious, crashing swells and breaks.

The surging gales even lashed at the colourless sands, once they had finished with the black water and rocks, and when the clouds succeeded, more and more often as the night wore on, in the absence of light, the entire coastline seemed to blend and blur into one treacherous mass. Merging together, it was as if the rocks and the water and the sand were all one and the same, indistinguishable from each other.

Deacon and Jen had stayed in the Grotto until the tide had started to come swelling in, forcing them to leave.

So distracted by each other, they had totally lost track of time, and only just made it back past through the huge stone archway, and up out of the narrow cavern, before the water engulfed the Grotto completely.

The whole thing, though perhaps dangerous, had been quite an adventure: exciting and forbidden, and most certainly something Jen had needed.

Soon enough they were sauntering back along the lanes, hand in hand still, laughing and joking. Some roads were lit, and some were not, and they were making their way towards Keepers Cottage, in generally, roughly, the right direction.

Deacon led, and Jen followed.

He took her a way that she no longer walked, and for good reason, but she said nothing of it.

Beginning to withdraw into herself all of a sudden, Jen barely noticed the tune Deacon was humming, occasionally breaching the gaps in his song by substituting words for verse and chorus.

But the further they walked, the less and less Jen heard him.

They passed a corner shop on the left.

Jen's heart began to race and fresh, aged fear pulsed through her body in fits and bursts.

They turned the next corner and, knowing it was there, Jen stole a glance across at the street name sign.

Memoria Lane

Deacon, of course, had sensed that something was wrong.

He had noticed Jen's breathing quicken and grow shallower, and felt the slight tremor that raced out through her fingers and palm, held so protectively in his.

Naturally, he clocked her sly glance at the street name sign, and though he was more than capable of putting two and two together, he wasn't a mind reader.

He could see something was bothering Jen, but as of yet, he didn't know what exactly.

"You okay?" He breathed through the night.

Jen nodded, lying of course, but she did not speak.

"Does it by any chance have anything to do with the dream you had the other night?" Deacon posed, and Jen stopped walking for a moment and looked across at him, her eyes widening a little.

Although, on second thought, she realised she probably shouldn't be so surprised.

She sighed deeply.

"Yes…" She admitted. "This is where we were looking. Over there…" She revealed, pointing over to the bushes off the side of the road, identical to those she had seen in her dream.

Deacon saw, despite the dim light, and even though it was barely noticeable, that Jen's hand was shaking, quivering, even as her outstretched finger indicated over to their left.

But then, as if on cue, a deep, threatening rumble echoed out above them, and Deacon decided it wasn't worth it.

There was no point upsetting her further over nothing but a dream.

"We're going to get caught out here…" He muttered quietly, glancing up at the sky with a frown.

Jen squinted upwards too, though admittedly only half-heartedly, for her concern was still on her worry.

Seeming almost to respond to his words, the first few raindrops fell from the sky: big and heavy and freezing.

They quickened their pace, but the rainfall grew heavier, and the droplets grew bigger, and the temperature plummeted colder, and within barely minutes, caught out by the sudden downpour, they were both soaked through to the skin.

"Come on!" Deacon urged, breaking into a run, still holding tight to Jen's hand, leading her down Memoria Lane, heading towards Keepers Cottage still.

But the faster they ran, the heavier the rain seemed to fall, and before long they were sprinting, hand in hand, laughing uncontrollably, absolutely drenched, as the storm pelted them relentlessly.

Finally they reached Keepers Cottage. Fumbling for her keys, Jen eventually burst in through the front door and into the empty hallway, still laughing, with Deacon in tow.

The house was eerily quiet as they slipped off their sodden, squelching shoes, and no matter how hard they tried to prevent it, they still dripped water all over the floor.

"Mom!?" Jen called out through the empty rooms. There came no reply. Not even an echo.

Only the hallway and landing lights were on, and even they seemed to flicker dimly as if they'd been left on by accident.

Jen followed Deacon into the kitchen, and there they found a scrap of paper upon the worktop, torn out of a notebook.

Sweetheart,

Gone over to see your Grandparents. Will probably stay the night.

Mandy dropped in again to see how you are.

If I'm not back before you go to work tomorrow I'll see you when you get home.

M/xx

"Do your grandparents live far then?" Deacon posed, though Jen thought perhaps that wasn't the most pertinent question he could have asked.

"About an hour and a half away." Jen replied, nodding slightly. "Whenever we go to see them they usually ask us to stay. It's easier, and they don't like the idea of us driving back so late."

"They sound nice." Deacon commented, smiling thoughtfully.

"They are." Jen agreed. "Maybe I can introduce you?" She offered.

"That'd be nice." He agreed. "What about Mandy?" He asked then: the question Jen had been dreading from the moment she'd seen the note. "Is she a friend of yours? I've not heard you talk about her?"

"She's just a family friend…" Jen lied.

Whether Deacon could sense her falsity or not, she didn't know.

He only nodded in response, pursing his lips slightly.

However, in brutal truth, whether Deacon had picked up on it or not, neither of them were really bothered about the note.

Her guard almost completely down. All inhibitions on hold, Jen felt a now familiar rush of desire suddenly surge through her.

Shyness erased, lost in the silence and emptiness all around, Jen practically jumped on Deacon. In turn, he didn't hold back either, lifting her effortlessly off the ground in a single, sweeping movement.

Jen wrapped her legs around his hips once more, pulling herself tightly to him, holding him immediately as close as she could.

Still soaked through, unable to help herself a second longer, Jen ripped and tore at Deacon's clothes, desperately wrenching his shirt off and throwing it anywhere.

He put her on the table top and in seconds had her dress up and over her head, pulling it from her drenched body and tossing it away without a second thought.

His hands began to explore her body, tracing their way up and down Jen's back first, down and round the backs of her legs, and then up between her thighs. His fingers danced lightly over her body and up to her full bodice, lingering there in a way that made Jen want to gasp and pant for air.

Jen's hands dove down to Deacon's jeans, yanking his belt loose and launching it across the kitchen. It clattered against the cupboards, somewhere over the other side of the room, but Jen's hands were already upon him, not even bothering to undo his trousers first.

With pleasured delight she shuddered as his hands explored her, and bit his lip as he kissed her.

Her hands did not relent even once, and they forced their way deeper and harder upon him as her desires grew and evolved, driving Jen insane through frantic, craving lust.

Deacon grabbed her thighs and pulled her up onto him, and Jen felt him press forcefully against her, moaning aloud as he did so.

In moments he was carrying her up the stairs, holding her close as Jen kissed and bit lightly at his neck, driven by something so strong that she had never experienced anything like it.

He threw her onto the bed and jumped atop her, their warm, blurred silhouettes merging together in the dim light, becoming as one in the darkness of the cold night.

Immediately Jen's hands once more found their way to Deacon's jeans, fumbling blindly to pull them loose. Soon enough they were thrown aside, and forgotten just as quickly, as her hands dove down and stroked him firmly with wandering fingers.

Lifting and moving her with ease, Deacon's strong arms spun Jen round on the bed, manhandling her in the dark of the night, and he pressed his warm, pulsing body firmly against her in the blurred, shadowy light.

Jen groaned loudly as she felt him rub against her, driving her mad, throwing her emotions out of control. She ran her hands up and down his back, passing over the ridges of his hundred and more scars, one by one.

He held himself over her, kissing her neck tenderly, working his way occasionally down to her chest, and then back up again, leaving desperate yearning everywhere he went.

Deacon's searching hands slipped down inside Jen's legs, gripping her thighs, making her moan loudly again and arch her back violently, thrusting her hips forcefully up against his body.

Then he had her on her front, moving and turning her without effort, as if she were completely weightless.

His hands danced across her skin, up and down her back, purposefully tormenting her, driving her crazy.

Before Jen knew it she was on her back once again, lost in the darkness as Deacon spun her with ease. And somehow, in the very same movement, he threw her bra blindly across the room through the darkness, for his hands moved deftly and had been busy.

But they didn't stop there, and his skilful fingers wove their way across her skin, up and down from her bosom to her hips, and Jen drew short, sharp, excited breaths, gasping as he navigated his way through her body.

She felt as if his hands belonged upon her, as though it were the most natural thing in the world; as though they had always been there. But that was not the only thing that felt natural, and as Deacon kissed her lightly from her ribs down to her stomach, he slipped his hands down past Jen's hips and along her thighs, taking all that remained of her clothes with them.

Naked and exposed, Jen pulled Deacon desperately closer to her, burying his head into her chest. And as he kissed her she pulled with shaky hands at all that remained of what he wore.

But it was not nerves that made her body tremble so.

No.

It was lust and longing.

It was a feeling that Jen couldn't control.

And there was no need for her to even try, for as her hands ran up his bare body, feeling his every scar, she felt him press against her again, now closer than ever before. Her racing heart skipped yet another few beats and she groaned in both pleasure and frustration, wanting him now more than she'd ever wanted anything in her entire life.

He pushed against her again.

And again.

And then again.

Teasing her.

Driving her wild.

Jen clasped both hands about the back of Deacon's neck, linking her fingers in his hair and pulling him down to kiss her. The trace of his lips on hers only made her want him more, and he breathed passion and desire into her with every touch, longing for each other constantly.

Still with her fingers around the back of his neck, Deacon entwined one hand in Jen's hair, and allowed the other to wander freely up and down her exposed body. And anywhere it found her, which was everywhere, his touch sent chills racing up and down her spine.

His strong arms reached beneath her then, pulling her closer to him than even seemed possible. As his hands slipped down and around the curve of Jen's back, she gasped and cried out, breaking their kiss for but a moment and burying her head into his neck, as she felt him slip gently inside her.

She groaned and arched as he held her there. Kissing her desperately, longingly, he returned her passion tenfold, grasping her firmly and tenderly all at once, pushing himself further and deeper, slowly and purposefully.

Jen felt every inch, and moaned uncontrollably as he slid up inside of her, sending her screaming.

Leaning in and out, slowly at first, Jen felt him bury deeper and deeper every time. But before long Deacon thrust harder and faster, over and over, and Jen screamed at the top of her lungs and clutched at him for all she was worth, digging her nails into his back and arms.

Deacon lifted Jen then and flung her over, spinning her so that she was atop him, and instinctively she thrust her hips down onto him, quivering as she felt every bit of him drive up inside of her.

Her feet wrapped beneath the backs of his legs and he drove his hips upwards. Jen shuddered with wild pleasure at every moment, feeling him so far within her that she could barely stand it. But at the same time, she never wanted him to stop, and she screamed endlessly for more.

The night swept by in a dark, misty haze of sweat and lust and euphoria.

Young Miss Jennifer Williams and Mr Deacon Ash revelled in each other for many hours to follow. It was only through sheer exhaustion, into the very early hours of the morning, that their aching hunger and their yearning desire for each other finally quelled enough for them to cease.

Panting heavily, drenched in sweat, breathless and drained beyond belief, in more ways than one, Jen clutched at Deacon, and his arms enveloped her protectively.

And there they stayed, shattered, falling into a heavy sleep that brought with it much needed rest.

Yet, it also unleashed wandering dreams, fraught with whole new experiences of their own.

Around Your Neck

The beach was grim and the driving wind whipped up clumps of damp sand in great flurries and flung them viciously at Jen's naked, exposed face. A crippling grey mist hung in the air like a wet blanket that weighed heavily down on the Earth, soaking all of the warmth and joy out of even the very ground itself.

There was no sunlight. Not that could be seen through the fog anyway.

The rocks in the distance were black; they were so black in fact that it almost looked like they had been covered in tar and left to seal, hardening and fastening coldly on the brutal coastline.

Even the very water itself had no colour to it, and despite the fierce wind, it sat still and undisturbed, without so much as a ripple crossing its bleak surface. It was as if somebody had stolen every ounce of energy from its swelling, breaking and crashing tides, locked it away forever, and thrown away the key.

If there were gulls anywhere overhead, or people anywhere around for that matter, they could be neither seen nor heard through the hovering blanket of solid vapour.

Jen's clothes were drenched in an instant and they clung to her horribly.

She appeared on the beach out of nowhere, or so it seemed, for in one moment she was warm and dry and comfortable, and in the next she was cold and dank and miserable.

Shivers clambered sluggishly up and down her back, and most certainly not the good kind, for it seemed she had gone from one extreme to the other, in every sense.

Alone on the morbid, grey sand, she glanced around nervously, as if she didn't want to be here, even though somehow she felt as though this was where she belonged.

Besides, where else had she to go?

She had made this her home, and now she had to live with it.

And she didn't mean the beach.

Suddenly a vast shadow loomed in the fog; a single, monstrous figure that screamed recognition at Jen and swarmed around her menacingly.

Jen cowered and ducked down to the ground, shielding her head and spinning round desperately, trying to keep the silhouette in view.

She chased blurry shadows and hidden memories that outran her endlessly, just like always.

The figure seemed to shift and change shape continuously in the fog, never assuming a single form that Jen could identify. Nonetheless though, she felt vaguely as if she recognised whatever it was that was taunting her. It haunted her in its ever changing form, yet it swooped around her in such a familiar manner that Jen couldn't help but be intrigued.

She almost wanted it to claim her, if only to allow herself to realise the truth.

By now she knew she was dreaming. But that didn't matter. Aside from the last few days that she had spent with Deacon, this sole dream felt more real than the past twelve months all combined.

For some reason now, in her unconscious state, she seemed to understand things more clearly.

In fact, she realised, it was not even that she hadn't understood whilst she'd been awake, instead, it was simply that she had been unwilling to accept her own realisation.

Now though, drifting amidst her dreams and lost in deep thought, her usual inhibitions were not so limiting, and that mere fact was quite uplifting.

Seeming to respond to her very thoughts, the encircling silhouette slowed its frantic flight, settling into a much steadier rhythm. It adopted a smooth, peaceful glide, and assumed a single, much less threatening form, though admittedly it was still blurry in the mist.

Jen rose to her feet, less affected by the cold now for some reason, though she was still just as wet through. She linked her hands and fingers in front of her and followed the shadowy figure with a calm, patient gaze as it slowed and descended and finally emerged from the concealing fog.

Folding his wings graciously into his sides and landing upon the damp sand before Jen with unparalleled grace, the albatross looked her dead in the eyes with its black, all seeing gaze.

Now she knew for absolute certain that this was a dream, for as he landed opposite her, barely three or four feet away, the albatross stood exactly as tall as she did. He shook a thousand droplets of moisture from his white and black feathers, ruffling his magnificent plumage repeatedly, only for the water to settle again almost immediately.

"Hello." Jen greeted the enormous bird, though her voice wavered slightly as she spoke for what felt like the first time in years.

The albatross cocked his head to one side slightly, looking Jen up and down with his steady, pitch black gaze. His long yellow beak, tipped with orange more vibrant than ever, seemed to curve up impossibly at the sides.

"Good afternoon Jenny." He greeted her in response, tipping his vast head slightly, and very courteously, just like somebody else Jen knew.

"Ahhh…" Jen faltered.

She had not actually expected him to reply, and now she didn't know what to do.

He smiled understandingly, if that were even possible with a beak, and gave her a moment to recover.

"I…I'm Jen…" She eventually managed to introduce herself.

"I know." The albatross replied immediately, without even the slightest flicker of mockery or ridicule.

"Oh…" Jen replied dimly, hesitating again as her wit failed her, realising all at once that he had indeed greeted her by name. "Of course…"

He allowed for there to be silence once again as Jen tried to gather her thoughts.

At last she seemed to have composed herself.

"Who are you?" She asked.

Her words were spoken quite pointedly, and with perhaps considerably less tact than she had intended. However, they did the job, and he didn't seem to mind.

"I'm your albatross." He replied quite simply, as if that much was obvious.

His voice sounded so age old that it seemed entirely possible that it might wear out completely at any moment. Yet, at the same time, his tone carried also the hint of lonesome youth that we are all burdened with for many years before we learn the truth about ourselves.

"Right…" Jen answered, in once more not the most impressive display of keen intellect.

Nonetheless, she persevered, and the albatross was amongst the most patient of creatures, so it mattered not.

"Do you have a name?" Jen asked next.

The albatross looked thoughtful for a moment, and glanced out into the thick mist pensively.

"You've given me many different names in the past…" He eventually replied mysteriously, though Jen had no doubt that his word was the unquestionable truth. "Though, one much more than all others…" He added as an afterthought.

Jen considered that for a moment and he looked on at her as if this point in their conversation was one of the most pivotal.

"May I just call you Albatross?" She requested. "For now, at least."

He continued to stare at her, his eyes penetrating deeper than just the mere surface, and that look pressed an explanation out of young Jennifer, for it was the most vital part.

"You…I… Jen struggled, but he pressed her still, not harshly, but firmly. "You're not like anybody I've ever met…" She finally managed, though floundering still. "So…I don't see how I can give you a name that anybody else I've ever known has…"

He cocked his head again, this time to the other side, and his pressing gaze relented, his eyes softening, though they were still jet black agates.

"Very well." He finally answered. "A sound reason. Very unbiased." He applauded her. "Albatross it is."

"Really?" Jen questioned, her brow furrowing as if she had expected him to reject her reasoning.

"You shouldn't doubt yourself so, Jenny." He chided her kindly. "It's not the name I expected." He admitted. "But, actually, I'm pleased."

"Erm…" Jen wavered, unsure exactly how to take that comment. "Thank you…"

What had he expected?

"Let's not worry about that for now." He suggested, and Jen gasped slightly, for she had not spoken the question aloud.

But then he gave her a very knowing look, as if perhaps she should have expected nothing else.

"Ah…" She finally replied, laughing slightly as realisation flooded through her. "I'm dreaming…" She stated, clarifying the obvious. "Of course you know what I'm thinking. You're in my head."

"And now we appear to be making progress." He commended her, his tone congratulatory.

"Thank you…" Jen repeated, and he ruffled his huge feathers once more, casting countless droplets of water off in every direction.

"Although…" He countered, looking at her in a strange, knowing and expectant sort of way. "We still have a long way to go."

Silence ensued then for a few moments, and Jen looked to be deep in thought, as if she was waging some sort of internal, moral battle with herself. Finally, sighing and rubbing her neck, she seemed to come to some sort of decision.

"Albatross…" She eventually started, and he looked at her with keen, black eyes. "Why are you trying to help me?" She asked.

"I'm just a small part of your imagination, remember?" The enormous bird reminded her then, flicking flurrying sand away that had settled on his humungous feet. "You're only trying to help yourself."

"Help myself do what?" Jen countered immediately, and Albatross's response came in just as quick succession.

"Acknowledge the truth."

"What truth?"

"You know the answer to that question." He reminded her. "You just need to admit that you do."

"But…" Jen started, before she paused for a moment.

Her mind raced, thinking how best to phrase her next question, for it was perhaps the most pertinent of all.

Finally, she came to a decision.

"Don't you get lonely?" She asked. "It must be very lonesome, flying out over the ocean for so long, all by yourself?"

The magnificent bird tilted his head to one side again, gazing at Jen intuitively. In a roundabout way, she was asking exactly the right question.

"Progress again, Jenny." He praised her.

She smiled in response, but didn't speak, knowing there was more he needed to say.

"Do you get lonely?" He asked her, his tone very serious as he turned the tables on her.

Jen thought on that for a moment.

She thought first of all, and understandably so, of Deacon. He was with her even now, as she slept, and whenever he was near her she felt safe.

But then she thought of her older sister, Clare, whom she had seen very little of the past few days, and the pit of worry in the depths of her stomach returned.

"I'm afraid that I would be…" She eventually replied, and the wise albatross could see that her words were incredibly honest. "If…"

But she could not finish her sentence.

He nodded slowly, seeing the pain and anxiety of truth in her eyes.

"How do you do it?" She asked of him then, her voice wavering and even pleading slightly, on the edge of tears. "How do you last?"

He needed barely a second to form the words of his reply, for they were indeed the crux that this entire conversation had been climbing towards, and the crescendo hit Jen with a wave of realisation.

Realisation at long last that, perhaps, although she was only trying to prevent herself from suffering the pain that would undoubtedly ensue, she was living a lie.

"I am often alone, but I am never lonely." The great albatross spoke to her. "I am constantly wandering, but I am never lost. I am forever away, but I am always home."

His words sunk into Jen's mind with the heavy weight of reality upon them, and she nodded slowly, holding back tears.

Her albatross took two long steps forward and immediately closed the gap between them.

He opened his vast, gloriously white wings, spreading them wider than she would even have believed possible, and cloaked Jen within them.

She hugged his feathered body and buried her head into his shoulder, as he engulfed her entirely within his grasp, and wrapped his wings tightly around her neck.

Breaching Barriers

Morning ruptured the dark, early hours of the day, and as the first streaks of yellow and orange sunlight streamed in through the window in the roof, Jen and Deacon stirred gently against each other. They were still wrapped up together, as they had been all night, and both of them were content to stay so for quite a while longer, with no real reason to rush to move.

Finally though, as the light brightened and glared upon their faces, they were roused to consciousness.

Jen lay on her side, tucked in front of Deacon, and she clutched at his left arm beneath her while his right draped over her.

"Good morning." He breathed behind her, in something that seemed to be turning into a habit, and Jen liked it.

"Good morning." She replied, smiling at the words and rubbing her cheek gently on his arm.

"Were you dreaming again?" Deacon asked almost immediately, running the fingers of his right hand slowly up and down Jen's body beneath the covers.

Jen turned onto her back and caught his gaze in the light of the morning sunrise.

"Yes." She answered, as even the very last tiny details of her dream came suddenly flooding back to her in vivid memories.

He looked at her deeply for a moment, drinking in her gaze with his.

"But not about the same thing." He commented.

Jen looked shocked for a moment, but then, she shouldn't have been really, she supposed once more.

"No, not about the same thing…" She conceded. "How did you know?"

"Your eyes." He replied immediately, as if the reason was obvious. "You have a different look in your eyes."

"My eyes?" Jen questioned. But Deacon's didn't say anything else at first, and he looked to be so deep in thought that his eyes glazed over slightly in concentration, though he still held her gaze firmly.

"It's something you've been keeping cooped up inside." He began slowly. "Your dream was reminding you that it's still there. It wasn't the same dream as you had before, but it has a very similar meaning. They're linked in some way. And, if I had to guess, I'd say the link is very important."

Amazed and astounded, tears almost stood in Jen's eyes as she soaked up his unbelievable words.

Feeling silly, she wiped her eyes dry, but Deacon tucked his finger softly beneath her chin and leant in to kiss her gently. She met his warm lips gratefully and revelled in his touch.

"How do you do that?" Jen asked him, once the seal of their lips had eventually broken.

"Do what?" He replied with a cheeky smile that told her he knew exactly what she meant.

"That!" Jen almost squealed, feeling her stomach fill with racing butterflies and throwing her hands up in mock exasperation, laughing freely. "Break my barriers! Make me drop my guard! Every time!"

"Why do you have a guard?" He asked her, tilting his head slightly to one side.

"Because..." Jen faltered, not knowing exactly what to say. "Just because..." She tried again. "Everybody does!"

"Not like you." Deacon countered, and he wasn't wrong either.

"Just...I..." Jen continued to struggle, but he was so right that she had nowhere to turn.

Deacon looked at her very seriously then, though his eyes were kind and caring as always. Jen could see he was racking his thoughts for something, and eventually, after a few more minutes, he seemed to settle on what he was after.

"Why aren't there any pictures of your father?" He asked pointedly, knowing that, if he was right on this particular matter, it would be better just to cut straight to the point.

He was referring of course, as Jen knew all too well, to the distinct lack of any kind of father figure in any of the photographs throughout the entirety of Keepers Cottage. There were countless pictures of the three of them: her, her older sister, Clare, and their mother, Dyra. But she should have known that he would notice such a thing, or maybe more accurately, the lack of such a thing.

He noticed everything.

Admittedly, Deacon was wary to breach the subject so directly, for he knew it would be a sensitive matter. Jen's mother had clammed up when he'd accidentally pushed her too far, only the morning previous.

He knew instinctively that there were things that haunted Jen in the same way, if not evermore greatly, and he didn't want to push her over the edge.

However, for some reason, and much to Deacon's pleasant surprise, without even a second thought, Jen delved miraculously into an explanation.

Perhaps he was breaking down even bigger barriers than Jen had originally let on.

Either way, he wasn't complaining.

"My father left a long time ago." Jen explained coldly. "He walked out on us."

"I'm sorry." Deacon replied softly, filling the silence Jen left in her wake.

"Don't be." She retorted immediately. "I wish he'd left sooner."

There was furious anger in Jen's tone that Deacon had never heard in her voice before, and it saddened him greatly.

"He was a bit of a drunk, but he was more of an arse." She spat venomously.

"Oh…" Deacon mouthed, but there wasn't chance for anything else, as Jen's ranting fury escalated.

"He just wanted to live his own life! He didn't care about us! He didn't want anything to do with us! He's never wanted anything to do with us!!"

Jen writhed beneath the duvet and lifted from where she rested upon Deacon in sheer irritation.

"Why!?" She demanded, though not really of Deacon in particular. "Why didn't he care!? Why weren't we good enough for him!?"

"Jen…" Deacon attempted, but her tongue lashed out once again, cutting him off sharply.

"And then! Even on the rare occasion when he actually bothered to see us! We'd sit and wait for him for hours! Bloody hours!" Her voice rose in a lifting crescendo, spiralling out of control. "When he eventually showed! Half the time drunk!! He'd just fob us off!! EVERY BLOODY TIME!!"

"Jen…" Deacon tried again desperately, this time managing to catch her attention and subdue her surging frustration.

She collapsed back into his arms and shuddered frantically, taking deep, controlled breaths.

"And every time…" She pressed on, by now needing to get what was left out of her system, for it had sat there for so long, just waiting to burst.

Her voice was barely a whisper, and her words rasped harshly.

"Every time, no matter how much it crushed me, I always just kept going back to him. Without fail. I always had more faith in him. I always had more love for him. Wasted. All of it. Wasted…"

"You loved him." Deacon breathed, and Jen knew he wasn't wrong.

"I did." She admitted. "But it wasn't my fault."

"No." He agreed. "It wasn't."

Jen laughed then in futility, shaking her head as another memory sprung into her overcrowded mind.

"I still apologised though!" She told him, unable to believe even her own words.

"Apologised?" Deacon question, confused. "What for?"

"I have absolutely no idea!!" Jen declared, throwing her arms up again, completely at a loss with herself. "Because I thought I'd done something wrong!? Because I felt like I was to blame!? I haven't a clue!!"

"Well it wasn't your fault." Deacon assured her firmly, and she held him tightly.

"I know that now." She whispered. "But I didn't back then."

Deacon nodded sombrely, understanding her pain perhaps better than most ever would.

"He finally left when Clare and I were eleven." Jen told him then. "But it had been going on for a long time…" She sighed regretfully. "Far too long…"

"You were too young…" Deacon tried to ease her pain.

His company was more comfort than words could ever possibly be, but he spoke them nonetheless, not one to go without trying.

"There wasn't anything you could do…"

"I know…" Jen agreed, nodding sombrely, though she didn't sound convinced.

"Have you heard from him since?" He asked then, but even as he spoke he realised that he already knew the answer to that question.

Jen shook her head slowly.

"I've thought about it." She admitted quietly. "About trying to get back in touch with him…"

"But…"

She thought for a moment, but only a moment. "He's not worth it."

The barefaced honesty in her voice then spoke volumes more than words would ever be able to, and Deacon understood that feeling entirely, and respected Jen wholly for it.

It was a difficult sacrifice to make.

For as long as he could remember, all he had ever wanted was to leave his life and his family behind, and start a new chapter: begin afresh.

It is a big decision, and indeed a saddening one, to want to leave everything you have ever known behind; to forget it, as if it have never even happened.

The desire to be somewhere unfamiliar, with people you have never met, and to see things you have never laid eyes upon, is perhaps one of the biggest drives that a human being can ever be pulled by, and it is most certainly not something to be taken light heartedly.

In the end, one day, desire always wins.

Eventually someday, sooner or later, it grows to be too strong. Old so called family and friends can all be forgotten, and the world can change beneath our feet in a heartbeat.

If you want it enough, desire always becomes reality.

"It doesn't matter now though…" Jen said finally.

"Why's that?" Deacon questioned, his eyes narrowing slightly.

"If he doesn't care, why should I?" Jen proposed, and quite rightly so.

"But you do care, Jen." Deacon countered, pointing out the obvious. Unfortunately for her, he wasn't wrong.

"I know." She sighed, burying her head into his shoulder.

Deacon smiled empathetically.

"Don't stop caring." He said quietly, kissing her gently on her forehead. "But don't let it consume you. Just try to care about the people who matter. It doesn't matter if they're family or not. Care about the ones you love, and who love you."

Jen looked deeply into Deacon's eyes, and they were filled with the honesty of painful experience.

"Those who don't deserve your love, those who don't earn it, they can be left behind just as quickly as they arrived."

He smiled lovingly at her.

"Your mom, your sister…" He continued. "They love you…"

But, as he spoke, even though Jen agreed with every word that he breathed, Deacon saw something change in her eyes.

They flickered painfully at the mention of her sister.

The thought of Clare drove instant hurt into the very heart of Jen's deep gaze. However, and not for the first time, Deacon couldn't put his finger on the reason for such anguish, at the mere mention of someone who Jen loved so dearly.

"And what about you?" Jen asked then, smiling affectionately through the agony that she was so obviously trying to hide.

"Me?" Deacon questioned, raising his eyebrows enquiringly.

"Am I allowed to care about you?" She asked, taking yet another giant leap of faith.

This was becoming something of a habit, and, if she wasn't very careful, one of these days she was going to fall.

"Well…" He replied, smirking cheekily at her.

"Well what…?" She asked, grinning back mischievously.

"Well I don't see why not…" He put forward, flashing his all-encompassing eyes upon her in all their glory. "I do love you after all." He confessed to her, breaching perhaps the biggest barrier of all.

Deacon kissed Jen then and breathed life and love and passion into her once again.

"I love you too." She whispered in return, taking a deep, shuddering breath, and the words rolled easily off her tongue as if they had been waiting there for days.

Then she kissed him again, placing her hands tenderly to the sides of his face and cupping his soft, stubbly cheeks.

Her heart raced afresh and she knew in that moment, beyond all else, that hopefully one day, eventually, everything would be alright again.

Hard Truths

Deacon left that same morning to go and collect his car from where he had abandoned it, parked by the bay. Jen had work that afternoon at The Rusty Oak, and he'd said he had work to do too.

Jen was just stepping out of the shower, wringing the worst of the water out of her hair with a towel, when a familiar voice startled her, making her nearly jump out of her skin.

"Long time no see, Jenny." Clare's voice sounded from across the room, carrying an icy hint to its tone as she spoke.

"Oh my God!" Jen gasped, snapping her head up to see her older sister standing in the doorway, leaning casually against the wall in blue jeans and a bright yellow T-shirt, her arms folded in a most dissatisfied manner.

It took Jen a moment to compose herself.

"You scared the life out of me Clare!" She finally managed, quieting her skipping heart.

"Not yet." Clare replied in a stony voice with an entirely unreadable expression, her words strange. "Not quite."

Jen looked at her older sister suspiciously.

Something wasn't right.

"What's wrong?" She asked instinctively, presuming whatever it was that was bothering Clare, she would tell her.

But it seemed that was not the case.

Albatross

"You look well." Clare commented then, eyeing her younger sister purposefully, and even somewhat menacingly.

"Ermm, thank you..." Jen replied, smiling warily as she covered her naked body with her towel, wrapping it round herself so that Clare could not see.

Indeed, she did look very well.

She had been eating, she had been active; her figure was returning.

She had been happy.

"It wasn't a compliment." Clare replied harshly, and before her younger sister even had chance to consider a response, she uncrossed her arms and slipped through the doorway and out of sight, making not a sound as she left.

Jen was left standing with her mouth slightly agape in shock, clutching at her towel that was wrapped round her still, dripping water on the cold, laminated floor.

That had come as quite the surprise, and Jen had absolutely no idea how to react.

"Cl...Clare...!" She eventually called after her sister, staggering to the bathroom doorway and glancing around, but Clare was nowhere to be seen or heard.

Jen had been abandoned, it seemed, and a wave of guilt flushed over her, rightly or wrongly so. But the guilt she felt was for many different things, and she couldn't help but allow it to eat away at her.

"I can't believe you!" Clare yelled at her sister, about an hour or so later, raising her voice perhaps louder than she'd intended.

But then again, perhaps not.

Clouds swarmed above as Clare ranted.

That morning had brought with it surging downpours that had left the fields and the beaches soaked through. As Jen walked water sloshed around her shoes and the ground squelched beneath her feet.

Though the ground was saturated, it was no longer raining, but still, an entirely different type of downpour barraged Jen during that walk to The Rusty Oak, as she tried desperately to fend off her older sister's abuse.

"What!?" Jen implored, spreading her hands defensively and almost even flinching at Clare's words.

"You're being ridiculous!" Clare demanded, as if that explained everything. "Are you being a bitch on purpose!? Don't I mean anything to you!?"

"What!? Clare! No…" Jen tried to justify to her sister, but Clare was having none of it.

"I don't really care what you've got to say!" She declared. "I know exactly what's going through that head of yours!"

Naturally.

"It's not even been a week!" She pressed cruelly. "He appears, and all of a sudden I mean absolutely jack!!"

"No…Clare…" Jen attempted futilely, but it was no use.

"You've changed, Jenny." Clare warned, her words growing grave and ominous. "You're not the same. He's been around barely a few days, and already you're a different person."

Finally, Jen had had enough.

Albatross

"Maybe it's for the better…" She bit back at Clare.

Though there was fight, and even truth, in her words, there was not the same spite, and she was still timid in Clare's presence, especially when she was on one like this.

"OH!" Clare exclaimed. "Really!? Is that what you think is it!?" Her eyes bore into her younger sister cruelly and her words spat venomously through the damp air.

"I…" Jen started timidly, her fear of upsetting Clare further getting the better of her.

But her older sister didn't let her finish.

"FINE!!" Clare shrieked brashly. "If that's how you feel, then I want no more to do with you!!"

And with that Clare whipped round, spinning instantly on her heel, and stormed away, back towards Keepers Cottage.

"But…" Jen's words trailed off, failing her as dejection set in as she watched her sister leave her, and not for the first time.

It was no good.

She just kept screwing everything up.

Surely it would only be a matter of time before Deacon realised that, and then he would leave her too.

But then, in only a matter of moments, out of nowhere, for Jen hadn't seen her return, Clare was in her face once again. She pressed her nose right up to Jen's, barely inches away, boring her angry gaze into hers, and breathed words at her dripping in molten hatred.

"What are you going to do now then, sis!?" She hissed through bared teeth, her features animalistic as anger surged through her.

Jen had never seen her sister so livid, and it terrified her. Although, not more than the prospect of her leaving again.

"What do you mean?" Jen managed, flinching back.

Clare wouldn't relent.

"What are you going to do about Deacon!?" Clare pressed cruelly.

Jen's answer was reactive and immediate, and she barely thought about her words before they rolled off her tongue, for this answer at least came very naturally to her.

"Whatever feels right…" She replied in an instant, as if the answer was obvious.

"NO! You idiot!" Clare berated her. "That's not what I mean!"

"What then!?" Jen begged, desperately craning her neck and body back away from her older sister, but Clare clutched at her tightly and wouldn't let her go, even though she couldn't touch her physically.

"You know what I mean…" She insisted quietly, brutally, her voice a threatening growl and her eyes hard and stern, forceful.

"I…I can't…" Jen stammered, indeed knowing exactly what Clare meant.

"You have to." Clare breathed, cutting off any other option.

"I already told him about dad leaving us!" Jen protested then, as if Clare was asking of her something she'd already done.

"No one cares about that!" Clare exclaimed, releasing Jen suddenly from her invisible grasp and throwing her arms up in exasperation.

Jen recovered slightly, straightening, though she still took a few wary steps back, and the clouds above circled in over her head.

"He was an arse!!" Clare declared. "You hate him! So what!?"

Her words were harsh, though not really all that far from the truth, but Clare would not let up, and she barraged Jen yet even further.

"That's not important!" She yelled. "You have to tell Deacon everything! And I mean the truth about what's really going on! Not just some dead and buried news about some arsehole father!!"

"But I…" Jen weakened, her voice dropping, and Clare interrupted again.

"BUT YOU WHAT!?" She practically screamed. "BUT YOU CAN'T!? You already told him one dead and buried story!! Now tell him the other one!!"

"I can't…" Jen almost cried, her will breaking beneath Clare's wrath.

"YOU HAVE TO!!" Clare shrieked, reaching entirely new octaves. "HE NEEDS TO KNOW!!"

"STOP IT!!" Jen screamed, shattering entirely, covering her ears to block out Clare's cruel words, but of course it made no difference.

She sprinted off towards The Rusty Oak, desperate for salvation from her older sister.

Desperate for salvation from everything.

But Clare pursued her, not even needing to run to keep pace with her.

Jenny would never escape.

The Rusty Oak came into view as Jen ran, her legs churning and her heart racing, driven by fear and by adrenaline.

Warm and welcoming amidst the grey haze of the heavy air hanging all around, and the clouds flooding overhead, Jen didn't let up even once as she stormed towards the rustic inn.

"JENNY!!" Clare called again, just as her younger sister burst through the heavy, wooden front door to the pub. "You haven't got a choice!!"

"LEAVE ME ALONE!!" Jen cried as she exploded into the foyer of The Rusty Oak, and all heads turned and eyes snapped to her in an instant.

She hadn't thought about that…

How on Earth was she going to explain this?

"He'll find out eventually!" Jen heard Clare's fading voice call through the slowly closing door, but her attention was no longer on her sister, as bodies swarmed around her in moments.

"Jen!?"

"Are you okay!?"

"What's wrong Jen!?"

"Has something happened!?"

A dozen and more voices fired questions at her. If she had not been shaken before, she certainly was now.

Flushed and out of breath from running, Jen couldn't draw air enough to reply to them all, and so they multiplied, growing in concern, and crowded around her even further still.

"Are you hurt!?"

"Is someone chasing you!?"

"Who was it!?"

"What's happened!?"

All of a sudden the flurrying questions, when they didn't receive appropriate answers, turned into decisive statements.

"Quick! Someone look outside!"

"Catch them before they get away!"

"Call the police!!"

That final voice suddenly drove Jen into desperate action. As overwhelmed as she might have been, the police getting involved again was the last thing she needed right now.

"No!" She cried, managing only a single syllable, still trying in vain to catch her breath. "No, no! It's fine!" She tried to calm and quiet them. "It's not that!" She reassured them as best she could, though, obviously, they didn't believe her.

"What is it then, Jen?" Laura asked her immediately, cutting through the teeming crowds like a shark parts the waves towards its prey.

Today she wore an angry, red jumper, and her words were direct and filled with concern.

"It's…I, it's not that…" Jen attempted, her answer vague and her voice shaky, though she was glad to be speaking to just Laura.

But she wasn't buying it.

"Jen." She said then, looking at her with serious eyes. "You must tell us if it's, you know…"

"No!" Jen almost cried, restraining her outburst right at the last moment. "It's not, I promise!"

"Well…" Laura considered, though she was clearly unconvinced. "Okay…"

The teeming throngs glanced around at each other nervously, unsure exactly what to do, all frozen in their tracks.

"Honestly." Jen tried again, this time a little more assertively, her breath coming back to her enough to summon a more convincing voice to lie with. "It's not. I swear. It was just one of my friends. We just had an argument, that's all…"

"Right, well, if you're sure…" Laura confirmed hesitantly, and when Jen nodded, as convincingly as she could manage, the crowd that had gathered began to disperse begrudgingly back to their drinks and their food.

But Laura was not finished with her, and she pulled Jen off to one side and through into the kitchens, clearly having only agreed with her to help part the crowd.

"What happened, Jen!?" She pressed, her voice a hushed and persistent whisper.

"It was just a disagreement with one of my friends." Jen lied again.

"That boy!?" Laura questioned then, and edge to her voice.

"What? Oh no! Not Deacon!" Jen reassured her, smiling as best she could, pleased actually to not have to lie about something for a change.

"Right…" Laura said cautiously again. "Well, if you're sure…I just want to help. You can tell me if something's wrong…"

"I know…I'm sorry I burst in. I'm fine." Jen reassured her, a little more convincingly now, for she had fully regained her breath and her face was less flushed.

Laura's eyes examined her one final time.

"Okay…" She finally breathed, but then her voice dropped to a hushed whisper again. "But if it is, you know, if you think…" She attempted, not sure how to phrase what she was trying to say. "If you see, you know…"

"Honestly, Laura, it's not." Jen said more firmly then, her tone suddenly more assertive, and certainly more believable.

"Okay…" Laura finally relented. "We just worry, that's all…"

"I know, Laura." Jen feigned a smile as best she could, hugging her briefly. "And thank you. But it's okay…"

"Alright." Laura concluded, smiling in return. "We're always here…"

"Thank you." Jen repeated. "But, please, try not to worry. Nothing's happened. It's not him…"

Lagoon of Excuses

Over the course of the next fortnight time seemed to shift strangely for young Jennifer Williams, and she felt as if the days passed by incredibly quickly, whilst at the same time the weeks dragged by laboriously.

Clare kept her distance during that fortnight, and though Jen often saw her older sister, she was always off a ways, watching from afar. They didn't once speak, and constant waves of guilt and uncertainty flooded through Jen at every fleeting opportunity.

She did see Deacon, however, as often as she could, and their bond grew only ever stronger.

But even by the end of the fortnight, she still hadn't told him the full truth that Clare had urged her so to reveal. Every time Deacon asked where Clare was, Jen was forced to come up with some sort of excuse as to why he hadn't yet met her, and the task grew harder and harder day by day.

Deacon may have noticed that something was bothering her.

In fact, tell a lie, of course he had noticed that something was bothering her.

But he didn't push Jen unnecessarily, knowing that, in her own time, she would reveal anything that was on her mind.

Much did he realise.
Little did he know.

Dyra however, wanting only to see the good, saw much improvement in her youngest daughter. Though it may well have been thanks to Deacon, she didn't really care what the reason was.

Jen was eating again. She was looking well. In fact she was looking stunning; her body had filled out in the way it always used to be.

She seemed happier than she had been in far too long.

At work Jen hummed and sang and danced and cooked and waltzed, and was more energetic than Geoff had ever seen her. It was as though she had been reborn, and was living a life renewed.

Nonetheless, as best they could without her noticing, he and Laura kept a close eye on their young friend, for they cared about her dearly, and dreaded the thought that something would again throw her off course.

Deacon often met her from work. He came to know Geoff and Laura well, and they both had to admit that they approved. The young man was polite, friendly, kind, and without a shadow of a doubt he cared for Jen deeply.

It was a pleasure to see.

Deacon regularly came to eat with Jen and her mother, Dyra, and he even painted for them one evening, and produced a portrait of the pair of them that was almost beyond compare. It immediately found pride and place upon the wall in their living room, surrounded by photos on all sides of both Jen and Clare, or of all three of them, though it looked somehow a little out of place amongst all the others.

Clare never made an appearance, however, and when challenged, that fact was met with constant excuses made for her by her faithful younger sister.

It was only those relentless apologies that Jen made which worried Dyra now, and Deacon picked up immediately on the fact that it concerned her, though he said not a word.

Something was still going on, something tucked far behind the scenes, he was certain of that much, but still he hadn't a clue what.

A few times Deacon took Jen out to dinner, and they laughed and joked and enjoyed each other's company long into the night. Once, he drove her a little further down south, and they spent the day on a glorious, golden beach that neither of them knew.

And then, one day, during the second week, he told her he was taking her somewhere else. But, when she enquired as to where, he only winked slyly and told her it was a surprise once again.

They drove inland from the coast, for an hour or so, and Jen recognised some of the places they passed, but then didn't know others.

Deacon liked to surprise her, she was beginning to realise; as is a man's prerogative.

Pulling up a narrow lane, barely wide enough for even one car, branches of bordering trees stretched out from either side of the beaten track and reached and clutched at the car as it passed slowly by.

On that particular day the air was warm and the sun broke intermittently through the rolling banks of cloud hovering above. The clouds were white and wispy, rather than grey and heavy, and tottered around their own ocean of blue without a care in the world, just watching the day while away.

Emerging from the suffocating treeline, crossing an orange strip of sun kissed ground, a lake came into view that stretched out into the distance, hugged on every bank and shore by the endless parade of trees. Jen's eyes widened imploringly as they wound their way up towards the concealed lagoon, abandoned and free.

"Where are we?" She breathed, though, in all honesty, that didn't really matter.

Deacon knew this, and his reply both remedied her question and left it unanswered, all at once.

"We're here." He replied simply.

Jen grinned at him thankfully and he smirked back cheekily, leaning in to kiss her gently on the lips. She ran her hands smoothly down his cheek and clutched her fingers to his skin longingly, as she always did, for she could never help herself.

Leaving the car, clambering over rocks and fallen trees across what looked to be the only clearing on the entire shore of the lake, Deacon led Jen across to the tranquil shoreline.

Tranquil as a mind without worry.

"Where are we going?" She asked him, following perfectly in his footsteps, fearful of straying from his path, for the consequences could be too grave to consider.

"You'll see." He answered her, again giving away nothing.

He crossed from the clearing and into the dense treeline, disappearing from view for a moment, leaving Jen alone for a brief second.

For some reason though, the instant he passed out of her sight, left alone it the silence of the undisturbed lake, Jen panicked, her terrible thoughts and memories rolling over her like a great cascading storm.

She glanced around nervously, admittedly, looking for her sister.

But, of course, Clare was nowhere to be seen.

How could she be?

Jen was finding that she was questioning herself more and more of late, and it was driving her insane. Things she had never known were coming to dreadful light, and things she had always relied on were slipping further and further from her weakening grasp.

"Got it!" Deacon's muffled voice called then from beyond the concealing treeline, interrupting Jen's spiralling thoughts. In seconds he emerged from between two stout pines, dragging something only just narrow enough to fit between them behind him.

"What is it?" Jen asked, recovering from her daze and moving swiftly to his side, afraid to be alone.

Her question was answered as he stepped back and out into the welcoming light.

It was a small, wooden rowing boat, old and well used, but sturdy and still in good shape.

"Oh…" Jen remarked, a little surprised, and her face lit up as Deacon stood straight and turned to face her, his breathing steady.

"Up for it?" He asked her, casting a brief glance out towards the water.

Jen did not speak to reply.

Instead, stretching up onto her tiptoes and placing her hands upon his chest, she kissed him. He held her there for a moment, his hands running up her back and into her hair.

It was only because she needed to breathe that Jen let go, and if somehow her kiss hadn't, the look in her eyes certainly answered Deacon's question.

"Let's go then." He breathed softly, his voice like rough velvet stirring the water in their wake.

Working together they dragged the rowing boat right up to the edge of the shore, leaving a trail behind them in the strewn pebbles and bark and dirt and sand, all mixed in together.

Jen jumped in once they had it half in and half out of the lagoon, sending tumbling ripples out across the water, disturbing its perfect surface. Deacon shoved the boat and it began to glide instantly out into the peaceful abyss. He leapt as he pushed and clambered into the boat beside Jen, steadying himself as the small vessel rocked slightly from side to side.

"Ready?" He asked with a grin.

Jen nodded, smirking back. She could never help herself with him. He brought it out of her like no one else.

Deacon reached down for the oars resting in the bottom of the boat, positioned them, seated himself opposite Jen, facing the shore, and they were off.

Dipping the oars slowly, rhythmically, in and out of the water, casting new waves out across the rippling mirror of the lagoon with every movement, he rowed them gracefully out into the middle of the lake.

A gradual, barely noticeable wind crept across the surface, snaking its way through the wafting greenery of the trees and tiptoeing over the water as if it wasn't supposed to be there. It tugged imperceptibly at Jen's hair, blowing it over her one shoulder, and Deacon took in the sight in all her beauty, even as he rowed.

Beyond her the surface of the water glistened in the dazzling sunlight, and the lazy clouds above seemed to part perfectly to allow it to keep shining.

All around the trees engulfed them on practically every shoreline, and Deacon even felt as though if the pines could have marched down and into the water itself, they most certainly would have done.

As ever, his eyes saw everything, and for that he was so glad, for he drank in the picture of Jen before him greedily, and never wanted it to change.

Little did he know though, there were certain things only Jen's eyes would ever see: things that neither he nor Dyra would ever be able to cast their gazes upon.

Jen stared out over the lake and thought of many different things.

Half the time she couldn't even put her finger on exactly which thoughts were racing through her mind at any one moment, for they flickered by so fast that she didn't have chance to focus.

When she eventually did manage to settle on a single notion, she remembered when she and her older sister, Clare, and their mother, Dyra, had gone out to a lake themselves. It was the one where they'd taken that photo, she recalled, that even still was framed at home.

It was just a shame that, now she was here with Deacon, thoughts such as that invaded her mind, bringing back her faded memories and her uncontrollable despair.

Still, Clare had not appeared, even though Jen dutifully glanced around every now and then to see if she would come.

But then, naturally, there was no way she could have been there.

Nonetheless, for a time, Jen was nothing if not distracted.

She fought hard against it though, and actually, in the end, in something of a revelation, actually managed to break through the thoughts and memories that oppressed her, and smiled thankfully at Deacon.

"Here, budge over." She told him, smirking as she stood up on wobbly legs and crossed the perilous two steps it took her to reach the board upon which he sat.

"What…?" He began, but before he could actually form a question, Jen nudged him over to one side playfully.

"Budge!" She laughed, plonking herself down beside him and blowing a raspberry on his neck.

Taking up one of the oars and leaving him to tend the other one, Jen grinned like a child let loose in a playground for the first time, and Deacon laughed merrily.

"Come on then." He joked, eyeing her with a teasing look. "Let's see what you've got…"

Jen felt like the more time she spent with Deacon, the more that her mood lifted, and the more easily she could keep her desolate thoughts at bay.

She felt so much more like her old self again, and she just prayed now that it lasted.

Surely it couldn't last forever, could it?

It was as if his very presence was keeping her devilish evils at bay. In fact, more than that. He was helping her, probably without even realising, to again become the person she once had been.

And with that: with her renewed strength, Jen felt strong enough to take on the day.

But as their perfect day wore on, the afternoon gave way to dusk, and evening laid itself out over the land. The tides found a way to change their peaceful rhythm, and order was stirred into chaos.

Speaking of devils, it was upon that very evening that a demon yet again came to visit the Keepers' household, and it left a devastating trail of destruction in its wake.

Dancing with the Devil

"So you'll both come?" Deacon asked eagerly, his voice full of pride and excitement and joy all at once.

Once Deacon and Jen had returned from their outing, Dyra had invited Deacon to stay for dinner. He had graciously accepted, for he was growing to like Jen's mother more and more by the day.

He found that she was a kind, caring woman, though clearly had also had her fair share of troubles and heartbreak. She had the look in her eyes that people often do when life has dealt them a most unfair hand, but they have no choice other than to just soldier on.

Conversation turned over to time Deacon's work, for Dyra knew very little about it other than that he was an artist. Jen had not revealed quite the extent of Deacon's success to her mother, and Deacon had in turn invited them both to an exhibition of his work that was taking place the following week.

"An exhibition?" Dyra probed, intrigue clearly sparking in her expression. She had always been a fan of all kinds of art, hence the photos, pictures and ornaments dotted all around Keepers Cottage. "What of?" She pressed.

"Everything on show will be for sale." Deacon explained. "It's a collection of pieces I've been working on for the past eighteen months or so."

"Oh how exciting!" Dyra exclaimed. "Is there a theme?" She asked.

Deacon nodded.

"Natural beauty." He told them, glancing with a brief smirk across the table at Jen as he spoke, causing her to blush, though of course that was by no means deliberate.

"Intriguing…" Dyra commented, grinning also. "Why natural beauty?" She asked without relent, clearly very interested. Deacon didn't mind in the slightest though. It was always wonderful when somebody else felt an attraction to his work.

"The whole event is funded by Greenway." Deacon began to explain. "The exhibition is called 'Greenway's Natural Beauty'."

"Greenway…?" Jen suddenly piped up.

She had heard that name before.

Deacon didn't cut in, for he could see her mind churning over, trying to retrieve the information she had stored somewhere in there.

"Isn't that an energy company…?" She finally spoke.

"It is." Deacon congratulated her, impressed. "They call themselves an energy conservation company. They're all about providing renewable energy, and looking after the planet while they do it." He continued to explain.

Jen and Dyra looked on at Deacon, amazed at his enthusiasm.

His arms and hands wove intricate patterns in the air as he spoke, and helped them to understand at least as much as his words did.

"They're in everything from power to nature reserves. That's why they asked me to base my exhibition around natural beauty, landscapes, that sort of thing. Their slogan is 'Green Energy, Green Earth'. It all ties in rather nicely…"

"So…" Jen started, her tone a little confused. "Why are they funding your exhibition?"

"I'm one of their biggest sponsors." Deacon informed them, speaking with a certain note of pride in his voice, and rightly so. "Half of the profits from the exhibition will come to me, and the other half will go to Greenway…"

"Half?" Dyra questioned. "That sounds like a large cut…" She sounded concerned, as if Deacon wasn't really getting a fair deal for all the hard work that he put into his art.

She wasn't, however, aware of exactly how much money they were talking about.

"Half is more than enough for me." Deacon assured her. "I've even been tempted to increase it. You know, give them a little bit more…"

"How much money are we talking about, exactly…?" Dyra posed then, wondering why on Earth he was giving away so much.

Deacon thought for a moment the best way to explain without going too detailed into numbers.

"Do you remember…" He started, speaking aloud even as his thoughts clicked into place. "When the windfarm went up along the coast…?"

Jen thought immediately back to when Deacon had driven her to his house for the first time. It hadn't been the first time she'd seen the turbines, but it had been the first time she'd really paid any attention to them.

"Yes..." Dyra replied slowly. "As a matter of fact, they were only finished just after we moved here..."

"Yes." Deacon agreed. "It wasn't really all that long ago. Well, they were part of the reason I moved here..."

"The turbines? Why?" Dyra questioned, not letting Deacon finish his sentence.

"Yes." He repeated, having been cut off before he could ever draw breath. "They belong to Greenway. There are fifteen of them out along that coastline, for now..." He explained before Dyra could interrupt again. "Greenway built them..."

"Right..." Dyra filled, desperate to get at least one word in it seemed.

"My last exhibition paid for five of them."

"What!?" Dyra exclaimed, though understandably so.

Jen's eyes grew slightly wide at the prospect. She had known Deacon was successful. But she hadn't realised quite how successful.

"And what percentage did Greenway get from your last exhibition?"

"Forty five percent." He stated.

"Oh my God..." Dyra breathed, realising now, all of a sudden, exactly how much money they were talking about.

"And how much does a turbine cost to build?" Jen asked.

"A lot." Deacon replied simply, leaving it at that, not really wanting to discuss numbers.

"So, what will this exhibition fund?" Jen asked instead.

"Well, that depends on if all the art sells." Deacon admitted honestly. "My last exhibition was a lot bigger than this one will be, but this one is higher profile. I think they want to extend the windfarms. I guess we'll find out when they get the money…"

"That's just…" Dyra began, lost for words. "Phenomenal…" She eventually managed, in absolute awe of what she had just learned about the young man sat so unassumingly before her.

"Why, thank you." Deacon replied, inclining his head slightly by way of acknowledgement.

"It sounds amazing." Jen breathed. Deacon grinned at her cheekily, as he always did, and Jen felt a sudden rush of pride surge through her body.

"It does." Dyra agreed. "It's one of the most generous things I've ever heard…"

Deacon drew breath to reply, but he didn't even have chance to do that.

Suddenly, and completely out of the blue, the front door burst open, rattling on its hinges it had been opened with such force.

"Dyra!!" Caroline barked in a disdainful, commanding tone.

In mere seconds Jen's terrible aunt appeared in the kitchen doorway, not having bothered closing the front door behind her, just leaving it wide open.

She wore a ridiculously big coat, fur lined along every seam physically possible, and nothing but a skimpy black dress beneath it that was undoubtedly supposed to show off her figure. Unfortunately though, there wasn't much to show off, and she looked as though she'd been on some sort of starvation diet.

Her heels were among the biggest Deacon had ever seen, and her face was a most repulsive orange, covered in so much fake tan that it wasn't quite believable.

He took in the bizarre sight of this woman who had appeared before them in an instant, and he disliked her immediately.

Also, he noticed that Jen's lip practically curled under as this impossibly rude stranger arrived, and pure hatred seeped out into the air from Jen's very being.

Dyra barely made it to her feet, and certainly didn't have chance to draw breath to reply.

"And just what do we have here!?" Caroline exclaimed, her words full of intrigue, but then also shock and disgust at the same time. "Dyra!" She barked again. "Why haven't you told me you've been having a guest!?" She demanded, eyeing Deacon with conspiring eyes.

"Caroline…" Dyra eventually stammered, but she was cut short.

"Oh don't give me that rubbish!" Her big sister shut her down. "Tell me who he is!" She commanded, pointing at Deacon in perhaps the most insulting manner that was humanly possible.

"What…I…" Dyra stuttered, and Caroline cut her down again.

"Oh do shut up!!" She dismissed her baby sister. "You're useless!!" She turned her head back to Deacon. "Who are you!?" She demanded.

But Deacon did not have chance to respond, for Jen leapt immediately to her feet.

"HEY!!" She bit, throwing her words through the air as if they were spears. "SHUT UP!?" She screeched in disbelief, going from zero to pissed in about half a second. "HOW DARE YOU!!"

But Deacon's hand on her arm quieted her momentarily, and her furious eyes flashed to him, confused.

He was on his feet and already moving. He took a step closer to Caroline, putting himself almost directly between her and Jen.

His stance was a defensive one, as if he was protecting them.

"My name is Deacon." He stated, though there was undisguised detest in his tone. "Deacon Ash. Who are you?"

"Who am I!?" Caroline spat in reply, as if she had been mortally offended.

"Yes." Deacon replied simply. "Who are you?"

"I am Caroline!" She scoffed at him, as if that told him everything he needed to know.

"Right…" Deacon responded, sounding decidedly unimpressed.

Caroline jumped to her next insult, seemingly faster than was possible, but she managed it anyway.

"What kind of a name is Deacon!?" She demanded, sneering at him as she spoke. "It sounds like a brand of soap!"

"Well it isn't." Deacon grated, keeping his tone as level as he could.

Jen could tell he was holding back and, in a way, she half wanted him to snap. Somehow she knew, if there was anyone who could put Caroline back in her box, it was Deacon.

"And how long have you been shagging her!?" Caroline demanded then, jabbing a scrawny finger beyond him and towards Jen, her bangled arm jangling as she thrust her hand out.

Jen fumed and seethed, but Deacon's touch quieted her as he reached back and clutched her hand gently.

"I think you'll find that what Jen and I do is none of your business." He breathed in a voice that declared war.

She looked stunned for a moment, taken aback by his defiance.

He pressed on, unfazed, taking full advantage.

"In just the same way that I wouldn't dream of interfering in your life…" He continued. "Exactly how many different men you have on the go is none of my concern, and especially not which ones are married and which aren't…"

Caroline's mouth hung agape.

Deacon's manner was artful, and he held himself with the impenetrable composure of somebody who had danced with the devil a thousand times before.

"You…I…" Caroline faltered, and Deacon simply looked on at her, pushing her back with his steady glare.

She eventually managed to recover, but the fire and the energy was gone from her tone, and she was left with only her distasteful manners.

"How dare you…" She growled, but Deacon was one step ahead, cutting her off before she could finish.

"Quite easily, actually…" He noted pleasantly, smiling frighteningly politely. "You know that scorn of yours is really most unattractive…"

Caroline's face turned bright red, out of anger or embarrassment, Jen couldn't decide.

She didn't have much chance to think on the matter, however, for Caroline's next jab was aimed at her, in a futile attempt at a comeback, lashing out in the only way she knew.

"So I take it you haven't told your boyfriend yet then!?" She gobbed at Dyra's youngest daughter, looking at her as if she was pure scum. "He's only still defending you because he doesn't know how screwed up you are!!"

Jen's face dropped instantly.

Dyra's teeth suddenly clenched and her big sister's comment forced her into screeching action.

"SHUT YOUR MOUTH!!" She screamed, lunging for Caroline with all that she could, hands outstretched, yearning, it seemed, to choke every ounce of life from her.

Deacon's gaze swept over it all and he tried desperately to keep the two of them apart, save them killing each other, for Caroline, naturally, responded in kind.

Jen jumped in to help him, ignoring Caroline's cruel words as best she could, focusing instead only on Deacon.

"WELL IT'S TRUE!!" Caroline shrieked in reply to Dyra's challenge. "IF HE KNEW THE TRUTH HE'D RUN A MILE!!"

Deacon didn't have time to think upon that comment however, as he struggled to restrain Caroline, and Jen fought with all her might to hold her mother back.

"He doesn't even know the half of it!!" Caroline continued, seething, though her voice dropped a little, for she was panting from her efforts. "You haven't told him what happened I bet!!" She yelled at Jen, pointing her cruel finger once again at the young girl. "LET ALONE HOW INSANE YOU ARE!!"

Jen blanched.

Deacon had had enough.

"BACK OFF!!" He boomed, shoving Caroline back, sending her staggering into the wall.

Had he wanted to hurt her, he most certainly could have done, but he wasn't that sort of person.

It took her a moment, but Caroline recovered.

"HOW DARE Y…"

She didn't get chance to finish her sentence however, for her baby sister, Dyra, didn't show the same restraint that Deacon had.

Careering around her youngest daughter and launching herself past Deacon and upon Caroline, Dyra swung at her with all her might. She cracked her big sister across the face with her fist clenched so tight that she could have crushed stone.

Caroline, having not expected it at all, went absolutely flying across the kitchen, and crashed dramatically into the worktop across the other side of the room, and thick droplets of blood sprayed across the marble surface.

Time seemed to stand still for a moment, as they all took in what Dyra had done. It sunk in quickly enough though, as Caroline collapsed to a heap on the floor, blood pouring from her very crooked nose.

"OWW!!" Dyra exclaimed, clutching her hand tenderly, practically doubling over with the pain. She couldn't quite imagine how badly her big sister's face hurt in that moment, though she hoped it was an awful lot more than her hand did.

Deacon and Jen stared on in amazement, though, admittedly, a satisfied smile crept over Jen's face.

How badly she had always wanted to see this picture, she couldn't quite describe.

It took some time, and admittedly, none of them went to her aid, but eventually Caroline gathered her wits enough amidst her spinning head to swear at them. And once she managed to get a few out, the rest soon followed.

She scrambled to her knees and looked up, still cursing, clutching at the worktop to steady herself. By now there was blood everywhere. Her nose was all too clearly broken, for it did not sit straight in the slightest, and the screaming profanities that flowed from her tongue were both foul and boundless.

Struggling onto wobbly legs, shrieking like a raging banshee, though they could barely discern a single word she screeched, Caroline staggered slowly forwards.

Had she been able to see straight, Deacon was certain Caroline would have sought revenge on her baby sister.

As it was, however, this was not like the films, and she only just made it out through the kitchen doorway, and in fact she still had to crawl most of that distance.

Caroline inched the rest of the way to the front door and out into the night, moving tentatively and uneasily.

Jen followed her with a certain satisfaction evident in her expression, glancing out into the heavy downpour with even more delight as Caroline crawled out into the saturated night.

Dyra's youngest daughter closed the door firmly behind her horrible aunt and locked it without even the tiniest hint of concern.

"Will she be okay?" Dyra asked then, suddenly realising exactly what she'd done, as a wave of guilt rushed through her.

Jen raised her eyebrows and looked to Deacon questioningly.

"Erm, eventually…" He decided, though he seemed in two minds.

"I need to help her…" Jen's mother panicked then, her voice wavering, but as she rushed to the door her youngest daughter caught her, stopping her in her tracks.

"Leave her, mom." Jen said firmly.

"But…" Dyra attempted.

Jen cut her off.

"Leave her." She repeated. "She deserves nothing less."

Albatross

Dyra nodded glumly and walked back over to the kitchen table, sinking down into her chair and dropping her head into her hands.

The atmosphere left behind in Caroline's wake was an indescribable one. It was guilt mixed with relief, a tad of uncertainty and a pinch of nerves.

Perhaps the most relieved amongst them however, was Jen.

That had been far too close to call, and had she had the chance, Caroline would undoubtedly have revealed the truth to Deacon.

Jen knew it, and when she looked into Deacon's concerned eyes, she could see that he knew it too.

He had seen everything.

He always saw everything.

She would only be able to keep her secret a little while longer.

But perhaps the thing that haunted Jen the most, as satisfied as she might have been with the punch her mother had thrown at her terrible aunt, was that despite her many faults, Caroline had been right.

Amidst everything, though her words might have been said in spite, or anger, or scorn, Caroline knew the truth of what Jen had been through. And in fact, indeed what she was still going through even now, and her aunt's cruel insults hadn't been far from the truth at all.

Greenway

Following that night of drama, things seemed to settle somewhat. Dyra partly regretted what she'd done, but then, at the same time, she'd only been defending her youngest daughter, so she didn't really feel all that bad.

Needless to say, Caroline didn't return.

She had probably made it home in one piece, Jen imagined. However, harsh as it might sound, she wasn't particularly fussed either way.

"Will we need anything else?" Dyra asked her then, yawning as she spoke, breaking Jen's trail of thought.

"I don't think so…" Jen replied, glancing around as if to spot anything they might be missing. She threw her gaze out of the kitchen window briefly and saw that the sun was only just thinking about breaking the horizon.

The day was young, only in its infancy in fact, and the clock had not yet even struck seven. Much too early, as far as Dyra was concerned. But then, she'd hadn't been in a routine for the best part of twelve months, and since in that time she'd not really ever had anything to be up early for, she'd gotten into the habit of sleeping in.

However, it was the day of Greenway's Natural Beauty Exhibition, and Deacon was coming to collect them at about quarter past seven, for it was a long drive to the gallery.

They lived right by the coast, which was lovely. However, to get to the nearest city with enough money knocking around for an exhibition such as this, the drive was always going to be lengthy.

Jen nibbled at some toast and cereal as she watched the second hand on the kitchen clock whirr slowly round, and Dyra cradled a mug filled with strong coffee as if her life depended on it.

Gradually the hands on the clock made their way laboriously closer and closer to seven, then five past, and ten past. They crept begrudgingly towards quarter past, and were a mere minute away when the kitchen window looking out over Shortberry Lane was illuminated by headlights.

"He's here!" Jen exclaimed. "Come on mom! Let's go!"

She was excited, understandably, and groggy as Dyra might have been, she too was looking forward to the day ahead.

Deacon had of course asked if Clare would be joining them, but, apart from the fact that Jen had even still barely seen her, she had woefully told Deacon that her older sister couldn't get out of work.

"Good morning!" He greeted them both enthusiastically, getting out of the car and walking round to open the passenger side doors as they came down the short garden path and out of the front gate.

He looked very smart in a black suit, a white shirt and a black and grey, striped tie.

Jen bit her lip when she saw him, and felt the fire within her throw out a few embers.

"Morning!" She replied merrily, planting a kiss upon his lips as he leant down to her, holding there for perhaps just a moment longer than she should have done, but she couldn't help it.

He grinned at her cheekily as she pulled slowly away, breathing a little more heavily than she had been before.

She looked stunning in her long, blue flowing dress, reaching down past her knees. It was something she hadn't worn for quite a while, but time had only improved her, and she looked positively ravishing.

"Hello Deacon." Dyra greeted him, smiling warmly. She too had made a good effort, and looked years younger than her actual age.

They all climbed into the car and were off in moments, zipping along narrow country lanes and out eventually out onto the messy spaghetti of motorways that are splattered across the country.

As they drove Deacon found that his guests still had many questions. He answered them all just as patiently as he ever did, explaining to them amongst many other things that once they arrived they would meet the Greenway benefactors.

Hopefully the gallery would be for the most part ready, but he would have the final say on any changes that needed to be made.

He'd done this a few times before; that much was obvious.

Dyra was more impressed with Deacon by the day of late, and it appeared that today would certainly be no exception.

It was several hours later, as the clouds traipsed along in the stiff, cold breeze, looking down upon Deacon as he chauffeured his guests through the colourless city, that they finally reached the gallery.

The building he pulled up outside of was an enormous structure, which looked to be made almost entirely out of glass, with but a few seams of perfectly crafted steel set within it that wound their way up its towering face.

An enormous set of steps led up to the massive, glass fronted double doors, and a dozen or so porters lined the walkway leading up to the foyer.

Above the doorway, etched somehow in black onto the very surface of the glass front of the building itself, read the outstanding title of today's spectacle, unmissable to all who passed.

Greenway's Natural Beauty Exhibition

Green Energy, Green Earth

"Oh my word…" Dyra breathed, as Deacon turned off the ignition and stepped out and into the chilling breeze, doing up the front two buttons on his suit jacket as he rose.

In an instant, less in fact, a porter was there. He was dressed very smartly in a black and red uniform, and looked to be no older than Deacon himself.

"Mr Ash." He greeted Deacon, his tone very formal and somewhat rigid as he stood officiously to attention. "Very good to see you back sir."

"Ben! Good to see you too!" Deacon laughed, handing the man he seemed to know his car keys. "Smile! Always so formal!" He joked light heartedly as he wound around the back of the car to open the passenger doors for Jen and Dyra.

"You're too kind." The overly official Ben replied, though he did crack a smile. "The pleasure is all mine."

"Oh stop it!" Deacon laughed again, grinning at Ben. "I've known you too long for all that rubbish!"

"I suppose you're right." Ben eventually cracked, laughing and loosening up almost immediately. "I have to try."

"And try you do." Deacon complimented him. His eyes and open hands turned to his guests then. "This is Jen, and Dyra." He introduced them, and Ben bowed his head in much the same manner that Deacon often did.

"An absolute pleasure." He greeted them both very formally.

"Ben here…" Deacon went on, shaking his head helplessly. "Is an old friend of mine…" He explained. "He's supported my work right from the start. Long before it became popular."

"I try." Ben smirked then, his change of character throwing Jen completely. "Deacon's done alright since then…" He jested, grinning impishly.

Deacon laughed and shook his head in defeat.

"You're a nightmare, Ben…" He accused.

"But you couldn't live without me." His friend pointed out, raising one eyebrow.

"That I couldn't." Deacon admitted thankfully. "See you upstairs?"

"You shall." Ben replied assuredly, stepping down towards Deacon's car to take it off and park it. "The bigwigs are all waiting for you." He grinned. "You'd better get your arse up there before they think you're not coming!"

"Right you are!" Deacon smirked. "See you soon!" He called as Ben restarted the ignition.

"Enjoy!" Ben shouted through the open window as he sped off and into an adjoining car park.

Deacon shook his head, but couldn't help but chuckle.

"He's a good guy." Deacon explained, as he lead Jen and Dyra up the steps and towards the huge, glass fronted doors.

"He seems nice." Dyra commented, and Deacon nodded in agreement.

"He is. But he's impossible sometimes. Greenway don't really like him. They're all about business. They think he's too much of a joker."

"What do you think?" Jen asked him then, and Deacon grinned at her even more mischievously than Ben had done.

"He's here isn't he?" He asked, winking slyly.

"You got him a job as a porter?" Dyra asked, but Deacon only laughed again, holding open the huge glass door for them and gesturing with his hand.

"No, no, he's dressed as a porter." Deacon corrected her, chuckling.

"What?" Jen questioned, confused. "He doesn't work here? But he said it was good to see you back?"

"He's never worked here!" Deacon laughed expansively, seeming not to take notice of the crowd of officious looking businessmen and women approaching them, and the sudden excited flurry of chatter amongst the beautiful girls sat behind the modern, mahogany reception desk.

Impressive statues and water features were dotted around here and there, attracting attention, as was their intention.

Naturally though, Deacon saw everything, and dropped his voice to Dyra and Jen one last time just before he turned to greet the encroaching throng.

"Ben's a nightmare, but I can't help but invite him. He's hilarious…"

"Mr Ash!" The man who seemed to lead the crowd greeted Deacon, shaking him firmly by the hand.

They were all dressed at least as smartly as Deacon, their blue and grey and black suits all pressed perfectly, but still, Jen couldn't help but think that none of them looked a patch on him.

Deacon made all the proper introductions, as he seemed to be all too efficient at.

"Greg!" He greeted the gentleman in the suit, warmly, yet still formally.

He was a very portly chap with an almost entirely bald head that couldn't help but be likened to a bowling ball. His body was almost as round as his head, yet somehow, Jen noted strangely, he wasn't fat in the slightest. There just seemed to be an awful lot of him.

"Jen, Dyra…" Deacon began. "This is Gregory Hughes. He's the man who makes it all

Albatross

happen." He explained, gesturing grandly as he always did. "Greg, this is my partner, Jen, and her mother, Dyra."

Jen shook Greg's enormous hand, but barely paid any attention to the compliments he showered her in.

She'd gone slightly giddy at Deacon's words.

Deacon smirked cheekily at her, though without letting anybody else see. He saw immediately the effect his words had had on her, and Jen tried to get a grip of herself.

But she couldn't help it, and apparently neither could Deacon, for the same thing happened over and over again that day, and neither of them seemed to tire of it in the slightest.

Being introduced as Deacon's partner stirred something inside of Jen that she had never known.

She felt all of a sudden valued beyond belief. It felt like such a long time since she had belonged at all.

No matter how many times she'd spoken to Mandy, or how much grief Caroline had ever given her, or how many times Clare had made her laugh in the past year, only now was it that she felt alive.

Soon enough, Greg and his studious, officious followers escorted Deacon and Jen and Dyra upstairs.

Jen was introduced to them all, at one point or another, but she couldn't for the life of her remember their names, and they all looked the same, she thought. The only one who stood out amongst them was Greg, and even then, he paled in comparison to Deacon.

Though, that could just have been Jen's infatuation talking, again.

Swept up amongst it all, Jen heard talk of past exhibitions and stories retold and old successes and new ventures since them. As the lift took them up to the very top floor, sixty nine storeys up, she couldn't help but get a little lost in the talk, coming thick and fast and relentless.

The lift pinged gladly and the doors slid slowly open, revealing beyond them a view across the city magnificent and unparalleled.

Directly ahead of them was the side of the building, entirely glass, save the two steel veins that Jen could just about make out running up either side of where they stood.

And then, all around them, on thick columns and pillars that seemed to be as much a part of the building's architecture as they were its decoration, were a multitude of canvases and framed works.

Some were painted, some were sketched and drawn. Oils and acrylics danced around for as far as the eye could see, some pieces so enormous that they covered entire walls from floor to ceiling, and others small enough to fit in a briefcase.

The art itself, varied and superb in a thousand and even more different ways, was unrivalled, surely.

Vast landscapes and unimaginable horizons, endless backdrops and deathly ravines, Deacon had thought of it all.

In deep contrast to the grey of the city beyond the perfect glass walls encasing them, this single, enormous room, seeming to revolve entirely on all sides around the lift right in its centre, was filled with reams of vibrant colour and life.

It seemed to capture the very nature of Mother Earth itself, and portrayed but the briefest glimpse of it here, all at the talented hand of one, Mr Deacon Ash.

It was fairly safe to say, Jen was in awe.

The Artist and the Impersonator

The morning and early afternoon were spent almost entirely in preparation, save stopping for an hour or so for lunch in one of the building's many restaurants. Great platters of food and drink were brought out for them, all seemingly at Greenway's expense.

Deacon checked and altered every inch of the gallery, with seemingly inhuman patience and calm, as a million and more questions were fired at him from every direction, and he handled each panicked worry with equal composure and assuredness.

It was all so alien to Jen that she simply held on as tightly as she could as she was swept along by Deacon's side. He looked after her and Dyra, there was no doubt about that, and at no point did they feel abandoned. But this was his world, it seemed, and modest and charming though he was, he was revered by all.

Continuing with the trend from lunch, come mid-afternoon, when the gallery began to slowly fill and swim with wealthy guests, food and drinks were swept around on huge silver platters by graceful waiters and waitresses. They navigated the surging and swelling crowds with apparent ease, collecting empty glasses and handing out full ones as they went.

Jen didn't recognise anybody who emerged from the lift, but from somewhere amidst the filling room Mr Gregory Hughes found his way over to her,

Albatross

and quietly and kindly talked her and Dyra through some of the appearing guests.

Deacon had been dragged away by a tall, demanding woman who had simply insisted that he must meet someone or other, Jen didn't really know who.

It seemed everybody wanted a piece of the great artist, Deacon Ash.

Jen wasn't jealous, she just felt a little overwhelmed by it all. She knew Deacon couldn't help being the centre of attention.

It was his exhibition after all.

Fortunately, Greg came to their rescue.

"That's Richard Brandy…" He pointed out first, indicating only with his eyes and a brief description, rather than making what he was doing too obvious. "Blue suit, tall, skinny, grey glasses…"

Though, everyone looked skinny next to Greg.

"Yes…" Jen mouthed, confirming that she knew who he meant, though she barely moved her lips as she spoke.

"He's one of our competitors…" Greg explained quite calmly. "He's not interested in the art at all, I'm afraid. He just wants to know how much money we make."

"Oh…" Jen replied, not sure what to make of that, and sure enough, as she followed him for a few minutes with her eyes, she saw what Greg meant.

Mr Brandy scooted from one painting to the next, without really lingering on any one of them as most of the other guests did. Instead of discussing them and looking more closely at the finer detail, he spent most of his time glancing around and eyeing up Greenway's staff.

"And that's the Lord Mayor and his wife…" Greg indicated then, and indeed, true to his word, the elderly couple emerging from the lift in that moment wore huge loops of plated gold about their shoulders.

"Are they here to buy?" Dyra questioned, a little startled.

"I doubt it…" Greg admitted. "We invited them to boost the exhibition's profile." He explained. "You never know though…" He added, grinning slyly, and his comment made Jen smirk too.

"Seems pretty high profile already…" Jen observed.

"We try…" Greg grinned again. "There's Amy Goodwill…" He pointed out inconspicuously, indicating a tall, slender blonde that had just emerged from the lift.

She was stunning in every way, and wore a knee length red dress that only accentuated her figure even more so.

"She made a fortune in oil, believe it or not…" Greg continued, though there was a yearning in his voice that was typical of the male sex, whenever such a woman passed by unescorted. "She loves dramatic art. Last time we ran an exhibition here she spent just over four hundred thousand…"

Jen started slightly.

"How much!?" She exclaimed, raising her voice louder than she should have done, and was forced to stifle her outburst with a cough.

"Smooth…" Ben laughed, appearing from seemingly nowhere and smirking foolishly, as if he was about to do something he possibly shouldn't.

Greg didn't really look best impressed by his appearance, Jen noted.

"Sorry about that…" Deacon apologised then, reappearing all at once from the growing crowds before Jen had chance to reply. "I couldn't get away…"

"Not to worry, Deacon." Greg assured him. "I was just looking after your guests."

"I noticed." Deacon replied thankfully, taking Greg's hand in a firm handshake, but even as he did so he leaned forward so that his mouth went to Greg's ear. "Mr Walker has bid on the ravine piece…" He uttered in a hushed voice. "Miss Clayton is trying to outbid him…"

Greg's eyes suddenly began to twinkle.

"Really…?" He breathed, perhaps much more enthusiastically than he should have done, rubbing his hands together as he spoke. "Do beg my pardon…" He offered absently. "This is something I must attend to…"

And with that, speaking not another word, he vanished among the thriving, ridiculously wealthy art lovers.

Deacon laughed.

"Greg loves a good bidding war." He explained, practically beaming at Jen and her mother, but it was Ben who spoke next.

"How much?" He asked almost immediately.

Deacon gave him a slightly withering look, but Ben did not back down.

"How much have they bid?" He asked again, though there was mischief in his eyes.

"So far, two hundred thousand…" Deacon finally replied, sighing, knowing Ben would not drop it.

His impish friend gave a low whistle, and Deacon rolled his eyes.

"You're impossible." He stated, though he couldn't help but laugh. "Anyway…" He continued then, looking Ben up and down in a most critical manner, for he was no longer wearing his porter's uniform. "What in God's name are you wearing, Ben?"

Jen and Dyra turned to look properly at Ben then, having not even noticed that he'd changed, and indeed his appearance shocked them a little too.

He was wearing a tweed jacket and trousers, rustic looking and well-worn, dark brown boots, a creased white shirt, open at the collar with no tie, and to top it all off leant slightly on a cane that looked to be carved entirely from tanned Birchwood.

His dark hair was messy and fell down in curls in front of his eyes.

Save that he was missing the pipe and hat, he could easily have passed for Sherlock Holmes.

Ben winked in reply.

"Ben?" He questioned, crinkling his forehead slightly in feigned confusion. "I don't know who you mean?"

"What?" Deacon urged, confused himself now. "Whatever you're up to, you're insane!"

"Not insane." Ben correctly immediately. "Eccentric!" He exclaimed, spreading his arms wide dramatically and jigging round his cane like a lunatic.

"Eccentric?" Deacon replied disbelievingly. "Why on Earth…?"

But Ben didn't let him finish.

"Because! My dear friend!" Ben practically bellowed. "All the greatest artists are eccentric! And yours truly is the finest of them all! The cream of the crop!" His voice wove in great undulating tones, rising and falling, well, eccentrically.

Jen and Dyra smirked as Deacon just looked on incredulously. He knew where this was going, he just couldn't quite believe it.

"Yours truly…?" Deacon started slowly, wondering whether he dare even finish his sentence.

There was nothing else for it, and Ben hung on by a thread, ready to burst with mischievous excitement.

"Who might be…?" Deacon finished, releasing Ben from his build up.

"Yours truly!" He exclaimed melodramatically, fighting immensely hard to keep a straight face. "Ash! Deacon Ash!"

"Of course you are…" Deacon replied, laughing and shaking his head as if all hope was lost.

"Now, if you'll excuse me…" Ben continued then, scanning the crowd before them briefly. "As the most prestigious man in the room! I have a conquest to make!"

"A conquest?" Deacon queried, but it was too late. Ben was off, cane and all, on a mission, it would seem.

Jen laughed aloud all of a sudden, struggling to contain herself.

"I think he's going after Amy Goodwill!" She hissed in a frantic, hushed whisper, watching as Ben chased down the stunning blonde in his new identity.

Deacon chuckled and shook his head yet again.

"Good luck to him." He mouthed. "I've heard she's rather feisty…"

"What will she do if she finds out?" Dyra asked, finding her tongue suddenly amidst the overly civilised chaos.

"Probably nothing good…" Deacon noted. "And it wouldn't be the first time one of his schemes has backfired…"

Still though, regardless of where they were or what the occasion was, Deacon had to hand it to Ben, for he was nothing if not persistent. How he managed to pull some of the stunts he did and still walked away unscathed, Deacon would never know.

Arguably though, there was still plenty of time for it to all go horribly wrong.

The day was wearing on, and evening was fast approaching.

The enormous room overlooking the bright lights of the city was filled almost to the brim now, and finery of all kinds was on show in every direction.

Suddenly, a familiar voice sounded from just behind Jen, and she and Dyra and Deacon turned to see a face that at least two of them recognised.

"And the lovebirds be attending the gallery together it would seem!" Walter Grimmway exclaimed in his exaggerated and overly flamboyant manner.

Jen was coming to find that most of the people Deacon knew were such, which probably spoke volumes about Deacon himself. Nonetheless, she was overjoyed to see another familiar face, and practically squealed with delight.

"Grimm!" She exclaimed, rushing forward to embrace the peculiar old man, dressed almost completely from head to toe in a purple suit and shirt. The only other colour he wore was the black of his tie and of his shiny, leather shoes.

"Well!" He cried in reply, taking Jen into his rough embrace. "What a warm welcome for an old man like myself!"

"This is my mom, Dyra." Jen immediately introduced her mother.

"Well! Well!" Grimm repeated, smiling crookedly, though somehow still quite charmingly, bowing fluidly as he spoke.

Dyra grinned and Deacon winked at her slyly.

"The pleasure is mine it seems…" Dyra replied, admittedly a little unsure of herself still, but growing in confidence along with her daughter.

"And what are two fine ladies such as yourselves doing in a place like this!?" Grimm demanded, grinning like an overgrown child as he rose his voice much louder than he really should have done.

He took a deep, exaggerated breath in through his nose and gasped audibly.

"It positively reeks of debauchery and corruption in here!" He declared, throwing his arms out in a grand, dramatic gesture.

By this point Deacon's head was in his hands, though he couldn't quite fully stifle his laughter.

"Why is everybody I've invited nuts!?" He demanded, words filled with at least half joking exasperation.

But before Grimm could retort with anything, Jen cut back in.

"I'll take that as a compliment, shall I?" She asked, smirking vividly at Deacon's helpless expression.

"She's got you there my son!" Grimm chortled, slapping Jen lightly on the back.

Deacon just shook his head and sighed.

"I can't win…" He laughed. "Now you're ganging up on me. What chance do I stand…?"

Jen grinned and stepped over to kiss him lightly on the cheek.

"None at all, my dear…" She breathed winking affectionately at him, and he took her hand instinctively. "None at all…"

"Attention! Attention please ladies and gentlemen!" Mr Gregory Hughes called, tapping the side of his champagne glass to politely hush the chatter in the room.

Gradually the subtle talk wound itself to a halt and all eyes turned to him, as he stepped into the only part of the circular room that could really be called the front, exposing himself wholly to the crowds.

Behind him the lights of the city shone and sparkled in the night through the evening that had encroached upon them so rapidly.

There had been a lot of talk of rather large sums of money thrown around that day; just the way Greg liked it, Jen imagined.

Deacon had been whisked off here and there through the day and night, but he had always come back to her, making sure he was never too far away.

"As many of you know I represent Greenway, and I would just like to thank you all for coming…" Greg continued, projecting his already gruff, booming voice around the vast room as if he had a megaphone. "None of this would be possible without your generous support…"

Brief applause followed his introduction and he glanced at Deacon out of the corner of his eye in that moment of pause, checking to see if he was ready. Deacon nodded almost imperceptibly, and Greg drew a deep breath to continue.

"I have the pleasure now of introducing to you the man who has made all of this possible…" Greg went on, cutting his speech as short as he possibly could. "He is one of our biggest supporters, and rarely do I have the honour of meeting anybody so dedicated to our noble cause…"

Momentary applause sounded again and Greg extended his arm towards Deacon in a slow, exaggerated motion.

"I have the privilege of introducing to you, for those of you who haven't already had the pleasure: the man of the hour! Mr Deacon Ash!"

Rapturous applause followed as Deacon rose to Greg's welcome and took the stage front and centre, shaking Greg's hand firmly as he stepped up.

He turned to face the crowd and raised his hand appreciatively. He was forced immediately to stifle an outrageous laugh, however, for away in the background his all-seeing gaze caught a glimpse of the ravishing Amy Goodwill, delivering a swift and effective slap square across Ben's cheek.

She stormed off and out of sight, and as the applause gradually died down, Ben just turned to face Deacon and shrugged as if he was surprised, grinning foolishly.

"Thank you…" Deacon began, though he was still struggling to keep from falling about in laughter. "You're too kind…" He managed, raising his hands again and buying himself a few more moments for self-composure.

He took a deep breath, glancing for a second at Jen and smiling shrewdly.

"As I'm sure you're aware…" He began, talking with his body just as much as with his words. "The money raised here tonight for Greenway will be pumped straight back into providing renewable energy sources for all of us, and for future generations to come…"

Another applause break ensued and Deacon paused, gathering his thoughts.

He didn't look nervous in the slightest, Jen noted. She was glad she wasn't the one up there.

"I would like to say a huge thank you to everybody who has made donations this evening, and of course to those of you who have made purchases.

I'm very happy to say that, thanks to your kind generosity, all of the paintings on display here today have now been sold!"

His voice rose and was matched by the applause and cheering of his audience. He beamed out across the crowd and Jen felt something that felt very much like surging pride swell up inside of her, and she realised in that moment just how much Deacon meant to her.

She only hoped that, when the time came that he discovered the truth, and learned in fact that Caroline was right, that he saw just as much as he always seemed to, and looked past the obvious. She hoped he would looked deeper into her heart than anybody else could, and when he did, she hoped that he loved her enough to understand, and to forgive her.

"However!" He cut them off then, glancing into the crowd at Greg as he deviated off script. Jen stole a look across the way at Mr Hughes, and she had to say he looked decidedly nervous at Deacon's sudden turn.

Clearly he didn't like undiscussed alterations to the plan.

She had a feeling, however, that he would be rather fond of this one.

"Normally..." He pressed on. "As I'm sure many of you know, a certain percentage of the exhibition donations go directly to Greenway..."

And even as he spoke, a young man in a dark blue suit, one of Greg's followers, appeared with a large, prewritten cheque, though admittedly he looked a little dubious.

Gregory's condition seemed to be catching...

Deacon took the huge cheque gratefully, glancing at the amount briefly before spinning it and showing it to the crowd.

Gasps of awe and overjoyed applause immediately broke out.

Jen's jaw dropped and she saw that her mother's did the same, as they both at the same time saw the writing and the figure scrawled upon it.

Eight Hundred and Twenty Three Thousand Pounds Only

£823,000.00

Eventually the applause died off and Deacon drew a very deep breath yet again.

Gregory looked to be sweating visibly.

"However…" He began ominously. "That isn't the amount Greenway will be receiving tonight…"

Rather symbolically he cast the cheque aside, dropping it behind a chair off to the side of the room, and allowing buzzing murmurs to start as he returned much slower than necessary to centre stage, grinning mischievously at Jen in a way that sent her weak at the knees.

"No…" Deacon finally continued, halting the chatter and silencing the room in an instant.

The whole building seemed to hold its breath.

"Instead, I'd like to donate an extra ten percent, on top of the fifty already given, to help ensure that we have our most successful green energy year yet!"

Jen had thought the applause before was impressive.

This time, before Deacon had even finished his sentence, the crowds exploded into a frenzy of cheering and whooping and clapping, ecstatic at his announcement.

Gregory too, Jen noticed, was overjoyed, and his panicked sweats had dried up almost instantly.

The speeches continued after that, as they were bound to. Greg joined Deacon once again and delivered an impromptu thank you, drawing heavily on his extensive vocabulary in an attempt to voice Deacon's overwhelming kindness.

Others came up to speak too, many of whom were among the richest in the room. And it seemed they had all donated vast sums of money to Greenway over the years, and had attended most, if not all, of Deacon's exhibitions.

After that, once the speeches and the many bottles of champagne had all run their course, the night began to draw gradually to a close.

As the hours pressed on and the guests began to filter out, Jen felt sleep beckoning her ever closer. She was exhausted, as was her mother, but on the contrary, Deacon seemed to be not in the least bit weary, and was as alert as ever.

In the darkness of the car, zipping by streetlights and bright signs as they hurtled home, the quiet music from the radio quickly lulled Jen into an exhausted slumber, all the while her thoughts upon

Deacon and his exhibition and indeed how immensely proud she was of him.

    Such thoughts to drift off to sleep to, for a change, were a gladly met relief for young Jennifer, and she welcomed them contentedly as the gentle rocking of the car cast her off into her overactive subconscious.

Unforeseen Shadows

An abrupt, harsh dip in the road startled Jen awake all of a sudden, and she stirred groggily from her slumber to see trees, fence lines, drystone walls, and the occasional cottage flashing by in the darkness.

She glanced back briefly and saw that Dyra was still asleep.

"Where are we?" She whispered, rubbing her aching neck wearily.

"About ten minutes away…" Deacon replied in an instant, throwing her a quick smile across the car, always so alert.

"Are you okay?" Jen asked, keeping her voice hushed. "Aren't you tired?"

"I'm fine, thank you." Deacon replied simply, reaching over with his left hand and entwining his fingers with Jen's in her lap.

She gripped his hand with both of hers, feeling his warmth radiating out even from that meagre touch.

He never seemed tired. He very rarely rested. Jen didn't quite understand it. But then, she supposed, it wasn't really a bad thing.

"I've had a lovely time today…" Jen mused aloud then, her words still very quiet and her voice low, as if they were just barely more than a thought.

"I'm glad." Deacon replied, nodding his head and grinning. "I hope so…"

"It's really something…" Jen continued to muse, and Deacon glanced across at her briefly through the dim light.

"What's that?" He questioned.

"You…" Jen responded without hesitation, and she immediately found herself blushing. "Your art…" She quickly corrected, though she hadn't been lying in the first place. "Your donations, your support for Greenway…I've never seen anything like it before…"

"Well, thank you…" Deacon replied, smirking so cheekily that Jen could tell even in the dim light the mischievous look in his eyes.

She couldn't help but flush hot under the collar, and though there was no way she could be sure whether he'd noticed or not, she had to assume that he had.

Soon enough Deacon slowed his car and they pulled to a steady stop outside Keepers Cottage. Dyra stirred in the seats behind and yawned loudly.

"Are we back…?" She mumbled in a groggy voice.

"Yes, mom." Jen chuckled in reply, opening the car door and stepping out into the cold air of the night.

It bit at her exposed face hungrily and had the feel of menace about it, even as it swarmed invisibly upon the three of them.

Then Deacon was by her side, holding the door open for Dyra, though he too looked stiff and cautious, and glanced here and there warily at the lurking shadows all around.

Jen's mother stepped wearily out of the car, grunting slightly as she did so.

"Thank you, Deacon." She managed, but he only smiled in response and closed the car door slowly behind her, his eyes everywhere all at once.

However, despite his keen gaze, he could see nothing in the darkness all about them, and the only thing that illuminated the deep night was the lantern that hung beside the door of their cottage. Dyra had lit it before they had left that morning, and now, for some reason, Deacon was very glad she had done.

Even a little light was better than none at all.

Nonetheless, he still felt as though there were eyes upon them, and the hairs stood up on the back of his neck, warning him that they weren't alone.

Jen shuddered and her heart thumped heavily against her chest.

"Deacon…" She whispered, her voice so quiet and terrified that he only just about heard her.

Her hands instinctively reached out and grasped at his arm, but when they found it, she could feel how tense he was, and that only consolidated her fears.

It took him a moment or two to reply.

"Come on…" He whispered in return, placing his arm around Jen and steering her protectively towards the lighted doorway.

Only then, already at the doorstep, did Dyra turn and realise that something was amiss.

"What's wrong?" She asked them, her voice piercing the cold darkness as if she had yelled her question.

But they didn't get chance to respond.

Suddenly a black figure lunged forward from the shadows, appearing from nowhere with huge, groping hands reaching out in the darkness.

Before she could get away, or even scream, horrible hands were upon Jen, clutching hungrily at her arm furthest from Deacon.

His grip was slimy and his fingers probing, leeching the very life from her just at the touch.

"It's been a long time, Jenny…" His disgusting voice slithered through the dark of the night, reaching Jen's ears and grating on them in a way that made her cringe and recoil from it.

The very sound of it made her physically sick to the stomach.

Time seemed to stand still.

But even as Jen tried to wretch, repulsed horribly, she let out a scream so despairing and desolate that she could have deafened a wailing banshee.

All three of them, Deacon, Dyra, and even the snake of a man clutching at her arm, winced and faltered at the ear-splitting, horrified sound.

Deacon was the first to react.

He had no idea what was going on, or who this man was, but he responded in the only way that seemed appropriate.

He doubled his hand into a fist, solid and unbreakable, and in a split second delivered a shattering blow across the man's face. He may just have been a silhouette in the pitch black of the night, but it was still more than enough for Deacon to see, and the young man's blow struck true.

The man in the shadows released his grip in an instant, and was sent reeling back into the gloom with a sharp, pained cry.

Jen's arm, now freed, found Deacon in an instant, and clung to him desperately, but it wasn't over, and he knew it.

He had to take control.

"Inside! Now!" He barked.

His voice was rough and his command firm, but it was on point, and the three of them piled immediately into Keepers cottage before the man, whoever he was, had a chance to recover.

Slamming the door behind him, Deacon whipped his gaze to the windows.

Dyra was panicking, darting all over the place.

Jen was terrified, silent and shaking.

"Windows! Back door! Check they're all locked!" Deacon instructed with no time to waste, as he turned the key in the front door and locked it. "Now!!" He commanded, startling Dyra into action.

"Okay!" She obeyed instinctively, racing immediately around each of the windows and the back door on the ground floor, checking they were all secured.

She soon returned, breathless and flushed.

"All done!" She reported, but Deacon didn't respond.

He was too focused on Jen.

She was sat on the bottom step of the stairs with her head buried in her hands, muttering continuously to herself, rocking slightly as she mumbled.

"Jen…" Deacon attempted, over and over. "Jen!" He pleaded, trying desperately to get her attention. "Please Jen…" He begged. "Talk to me! What's going on!? Who is he!?"

But Jen didn't answer, and she only hid herself deeper in her own hands, trying as best she could to just block it all out.

That's all she'd been doing so far.

But you can't escape the past.

"Get him away…" Jen whispered futilely into her own palms. "Get away. Get him away…" She repeated, over and over.

"Jen!" Deacon urged. "Who is he!?"

But then Deacon glanced up at Dyra, his eyes desperate, and he saw that she was ghostly white.

"Dyra?" He breathed then, knowing in an instant that she knew. "Who is he!?" Deacon pressed. "What's going on!?"

"It can't be…" She started, faltering almost immediately.

"Dyra!" Deacon snapped again, but it was instead Jen who answered.

She exploded up to her feet in a fit of panic and practically threw herself at Deacon.

"It's him!!" She cried despairingly, her voice croaking and breaking with fright. "He's back!! He's waited all this time!! Now he wants me!!"

Collapsing to the floor in a shuddering, heaving wreck, Jen's strength drained from her and her legs buckled, unable to hold her through fear alone.

"Who!?" Deacon begged.

"Oh my God…" Dyra whispered then, finally breaking from her trance.

"Dyra!!" Deacon cried, exasperated now. "What is it!?"

But Jen's mother was immediately on the phone, panicking even more as she called through to the emergency number.

"Hello! Yes! The police! Officer Mahoney!" She answered suddenly, as the responder at the other end answered. "This is Dyra Williams! I'm Jennifer Williams' mother!"

Deacon could do nothing but wait, holding Jen closely as she shook like a leaf, muttering to herself once again.

"Yes, that's it!" Dyra suddenly said, her breaths and her words fast and sharp. "We need help! He's here! He's right outside! He's just tried to take my daughter!!"

Suddenly Dyra hung up, as if she had cut the conversation off midway through. But as she rushed over to Jen, throwing her arms around her and sobbing aloud, she tried to talk through her tears.

"They're coming! They're coming, sweetheart! Don't worry! They're coming!"

But the cold, harsh reality of it all was dawning slowly upon Jen, and even as Deacon wrapped her up, still shaking in his arms, and she felt his strong heartbeat as she laid her head against his chest, she knew this was it.

She folded her arms up so her hands were by her shoulders, and his embrace seemed to envelope her completely, holding her closer than she ever thought was possible.

Her senses were returning to her now, very slowly, as her blind panic slipped away ever so slightly, though it could return at any moment.

She couldn't believe it had come to this.

Clare had been right.

Even bloody Caroline had been right.

Tonight, whether she survived or not, Deacon would find out the truth.

There was a cruel, ravenous knock at the door, and the sound lingered in the air longingly, reaching out for what it hungered for so dreadfully.

Predator and Prey

The man stalked silently through the night, keeping only to the shadows, moving as a silhouette slipping from one black crevice to another, leaving behind not a trace.

He was well practiced at this.

He had done it many times before.

Leaving one hand trailing behind him, scraping and knocking hungrily on doors and tapping softly on window panes, he knew the sound would drive little Jenny insane.

His free hand tingled then, grabbing his attention, for he could still feel the sense of her warm touch on his skin. Lifting his hand slowly, like a dreadful ritual offering, he ran his tongue along his aching palm, licking it like a wild animal, tasting Jen's fear.

The flavour sent his senses haywire and he growled deeply in the back of his throat, and the sound was unmistakeably yearning and insatiable.

Unable to control himself any longer, barely able to hold himself back as it was, he smashed his clenched fists against the door, shaking it on its very hinges.

A terrified scream wailed out from inside Keepers Cottage, which he had watched for so long now, and his hunger grew and evolved into something else entirely.

He knew what was coming.

He had felt it before.

And he loved it.

"I can hear you, Jenny!!" He called out, ceasing his hammering fists just long enough to hear her whimper in fear.

An evil smile crept across his face, hidden and disguised by the night.

"COME ON JENNY!!" He bellowed then, his voice deep and rasping and ravenous. "I WANT YOU!!"

With every sound that he made Jen winced visibly, jumping and startling and crying out in horror. Her breaths were quick and sharp and shallow, full of awful fright.

He battered and pounded at the door, rattling it on its hinges as if it were about to burst, and once again Jen shrieked like a howling banshee.

Her desperate cry was followed almost immediately by footsteps on the stairs, and Jen set shaky eyes upon her older sister practically throwing herself down the staircase.

Clare was bleary eyed, as if she'd only just awoken, and clattered down to her sister so fast that she almost fell head over heels.

Forgetting at long last the feud they'd had, she rushed immediately to Jen's side, desperately trying to calm her screaming.

"Jen!" She cried, but her younger sister could not reply through her sobs.

"I can't wait any longer!!" He bellowed from outside. "I NEED YOU!!"

Jen cowered away and Clare comforted her as best she could, ignoring all that he was saying and focusing instead on her younger sister, in absolute bits before her.

"YOU LOOK JUST LIKE HER!!"

That was it.

In an instant, Clare snapped.

He had yet again gone too far.

The sheer, vile abuse that she hurled through the air then, her angry words like sharpened razor blades were enough to curdle the blood. The foul insults that she screeched were not to be trifled with.

But, they seemed to go unheard, and the man stalking them from outside did not reply.

In fact, all went silent, as Jen and Clare awaited his response.

But it was an answer that never came.

He stopped shouting.

The door finished rattling.

Jen ceased her screaming.

In fact, everything seemed to come to a complete standstill, and an eerie quiet settled upon the cottage.

Deacon glanced around warily, wondering what on Earth would happen next.

Jen whimpered slightly, overtaken wholly by panic. Deacon wrapped his arms around her again, cradling her as gently and as comfortingly as he could, though he stayed ever vigilant.

Clare crept through into the darkened kitchen, making not a sound as she moved, silent as a ghost. She peered out of the window, staying as inconspicuous as she could, but after a few moments she recoiled gradually back, looking at her sister and shaking her head slowly.

Suddenly the sound of shattering glass exploded in their ears from somewhere at the back of the house, and Deacon sprung immediately into action.

"Wait here!" He instructed, darting through the downstairs rooms in the dim light.

His footsteps stopped, but before he could relay what he'd found, a large rock came sailing in through the kitchen window. It shattered with terrifying force and fragmented glass was sent flying in every direction.

Jen screamed again, recoiling back with her mother, both covering their faces.

Clare didn't bother.

The glass, like the cold, seemed not to affect her, even as it sprayed all over her.

Then, in barely a moment, Deacon was back, breathing sharply.

"Same at the back…" He reported, but then again he was cut short, and a huge bang reverberated through the house, followed by a sharp crash.

Instantly, Deacon whipped round and flew yet again to the back of the house, but he stopped barely halfway, taking slow, steady steps back towards them, still stood in the entrance hallway, his eyes wide and fearful.

The back door lay on the floor, its hinges buckled and broken, ruined.

"He's…" Deacon started, though, once again, he didn't get to finish.

A low, possessed humming echoed through the dark rooms of Keepers Cottage, casting fear into their hearts like nightmares laden with dread.

Albatross

"Oh my God…" Jen breathed, and her words shook and quivered awfully, her voice barely a whisper.

The sound seemed to echo all around, bouncing impossibly in every direction, and none of them had any idea where it was coming from.

An evil grating noise followed the humming, grinding with deadly intention upon their ears.

Deacon moved Jen and Dyra slowly to the staircase, trying desperately not to make a sound. But, as is always the way, that was near impossible in the dead of the night.

Still he had not appeared.

Pointing urgently up the stairs, Deacon quickly ushered Jen and Dyra to climb.

However, the first step Jen took, anxious and rushed, creaked loudly and obviously throughout the house, and in an instant he was there.

"GO!" Deacon bellowed, reaching out into the darkness and grappling with the silhouette of a man, fighting with all his might to keep him away from Jen.

Dyra forced her youngest daughter up the stairs in front of her, following Deacon's barked command in nothing but blind panic.

Behind them Deacon struggled against the man in the shadows, and Clare just stood by watching, helpless, unable to do anything at all.

The man forced him back against the wall, and in the light of the hallway Deacon laid eyes upon him properly for the first time.

His black hair was long and greasy and unkempt, falling almost down to his shoulders and partly in front of his eyes. Though he looked thin and weak, his grasp was strong and firm, driven by something more than just mere muscle.

But most prominent of all were his eyes.

Through his matted black hair his eyes were dark and fierce and crazed, maddened by something that Deacon did not recognise: some senseless emotion that he had never felt.

A low growl, like that of an animal, emanated from the back of the man's throat, and he was focused, committed, to whatever it was he was trying to do. Deacon didn't know exactly what that was, but he knew that it involved Jen, and somehow Clare too, and either way, he didn't want to find out.

Driving him away, Deacon exploded forwards and hurled the man back into the living room, practically throwing him over the furniture, sending him smashing into the low, glass topped coffee table.

He hit the floor hard and with a loud grunt, but in barely a moment he was back on his feet, unfazed, and surging towards Deacon yet again.

He prepared himself, and once more as the man from the shadows tried to fight his way past to get to Jen, Deacon proved to be the stronger of the two.

Three times the man tried to get past, and in turn, three times Deacon repelled him, each time inflicting further injury.

It was only at that point, nursing bruised and battered limbs, when the man realised that this young fellow, whoever he was, keeping him from Jenny, would not yield.

The time had come to divert from the plan.

Usually, that was not preferred.

And besides, he had been saving this knife especially for Jenny, as seemed only appropriate.

But, he supposed, sometimes exceptions have to be made, as he drew the long, thick handled blade from beneath his black shirt, brandishing it before Jenny's protector menacingly.

Deacon's eyes grew wide at the sight of the knife, knowing now they were in serious trouble.

By this point though, things had gone too far, and he had little other choice than to stand and fight; to defend Jen against this madman.

There was little time to think, for he dove forwards towards Deacon in barely the space of two racing heartbeats, driving his weight behind the lunging blade.

Jen screamed, trying to throw herself forward, but Dyra forced her back, seeing that it was already too late.

Clare looked on with tears standing heavily in her eyes.

The blade plummeted towards Deacon's chest, and triumph surged through the evil man's veins, tasting success, knowing that Jen would soon follow.

But Deacon was too quick for it to be that easy.

He had suffered the knife before, and knew its workings.

At the very last second, inches from death, he darted swiftly to one side, avoiding the blade by less than an inch.

Grabbing the man's wrist and arm, Deacon wrenched his hand under and practically jumped on the back of his shoulder, driving the man down into the floor face first, and very hard. The sheer impact caused the knife to loose from his grasp, and it scattered across the floor nervously.

His head was driven so hard into the floor that the man fell silent almost immediately, and his body went limp and weak.

Nonetheless, Deacon took no chances, having barely escaped with his life, and kicked the knife away into the depths of the kitchen.

Pressing constantly with his whole bodyweight, he kept pressure upon his attacker, not once releasing his wrist and arm, pinning him forcefully to the ground.

"Deacon…" Jen breathed, stepping slowly down towards him, relief flushing through her body.

"No!" Deacon instructed, and Jen froze, though his voice was not harsh. "Stay there." He told her. "Just in case…"

Clare hadn't moved during the whole thing, and she glanced up at Jen guiltily.

However, Jen didn't say or do anything in response, and suddenly, startling them all terribly, another loud knock at the door sounded.

None of them moved at first, their eyes transfixed on the sound.

But within a few moments, hearing a noise again coming from the back of the house, a concerned voice echoed through the darkness.

"Hello!?" It called. "Is everyone okay!?"

"We're in here!" Deacon shouted back, and within seconds two police officers came racing in.

"We saw the windows…" The first replied immediately, taking in the whole situation in much the way as Deacon always did, sweeping his eyes over everything at once. "And we saw the back door…" He continued, focusing in on Deacon holding the man to the floor, and the knife in the corner of the kitchen.

His hand went instinctively to his baton, though he didn't rack it, and only looked on for a moment, seeming to understand that Deacon wasn't the threat here.

A silent understanding passed between them and, all at once, it seemed that everything would be alright again.

Well, almost everything…

Decisions

What followed was a whirlwind of officers arriving and departing. Deacon, Jen and Dyra were whisked through into another room, while the unconscious man from the shadows was taken away and out of sight.

His awareness returned to him however, part way through the process of being removed, and he proceeded promptly to scream and shout once more after Jen, writhing and squirming beneath the heavy hands of the police.

His apparent insanity hastened his removal, and after barely a few minutes of the police arriving, though most certainly not soon enough, Deacon, Jen and Dyra were left alone in the living room with the remaining officers.

As the man shrieked and bawled, struggling desperately as the officers practically dragged him away, Clare couldn't help but watch closely, a look in her eyes totally unreadable.

"Jen…" Officer Mahoney started, sat opposite her in the living room. His huge, thick body seemed to perch on one settee, across from the young girl who looked so afraid, though his voice was gentle and understanding.

She looked up at him through fearful, confused eyes.

He smiled comfortingly.

"Don't worry." He assured her. "We've got him."

Jen only nodded, unable to speak.

The officer looked to Dyra and Deacon then. Dyra smiled, and Deacon could tell she knew Mahoney quite well.

He held out his hand.

"Deacon Ash." He introduced himself, shaking Mahoney's hand firmly. "I'm Jen's partner."

"Jim Mahoney." The officer replied, though a fleeting thought seemed to cross his face. "Pleasure."

"Can I assist at all…?" Deacon posed.

"Don't worry." Mahoney assured him. "We've been after this one for quite some time…"

He sounded as if he was going to say more, but a quick warning look from Dyra quieted him, and he changed tact slightly.

"Deacon Ash?" He questioned then. "As in the artist?"

"Yes…" Deacon replied.

"Blimey!" He exclaimed. "My wife loves your work!"

"Thank you." Deacon laughed nervously, but the compliment did little to lighten the mood, and fresh tension hung heavily in the air.

Mahoney beckoned Dyra with a slight motion of his eyes, and she slipped in front of Deacon almost even guiltily, for she knew he was desperate to know what they were keeping from him.

Suddenly, darting through with panicked but professional haste, Mandy appeared in the doorway to the living room. Her jet black hair that was usually tied in a ponytail hung loosely about her shoulders and flicked in the air as she came practically flying around the corner.

In barely a moment her dark eyes took in the whole scene before her.

It seemed to be an ability that everyone but Jen possessed.

Mandy saw Dyra with Mahoney. She saw Jen sat alone on the settee, head in her hands, body trembling. And she saw a handsome young man, whom she had never before met, looking very confused and torn between Jen and Dyra.

Nudging her glasses more securely back onto her nose, Mandy straightened herself and smoothed her black pencil skirt. Clutching her black portfolio case to her chest, she approached Jen slowly.

But the handsome young man held out his hand openly.

"Can I help?" He asked her, and his voice was hardy and velvety all at once.

"My name is Mandy." She introduced herself, holding out her hand professionally.

"Deacon. Jen's partner." The young man replied, taking her hand firmly and gently all at once. "Family friend?" He asked then, glancing for a second down at Jen.

She seemed not to have heard Mandy enter.

"Not exactly…" Mandy replied carefully, letting go of Deacon's hand slowly. He looked confused and waited for an explanation.

"I'm a cognitive psychiatrist." Mandy started to explain. "I specialise in trauma."

"Trauma?" Deacon questioned, for her explanation had not really shed any light at all, and suddenly Mandy understood why.

"I see…" She replied tentatively, looking very concerned as she did so, glancing down at Jen. "I think I need to speak to Jen."

"She's…" Deacon began, knowing that Jen likely was too fragile at the moment, but Mandy cut him off firmly.

"I'm afraid I don't have a choice." She stated. "I thought things were improving."

"Improving?" Deacon questioned.

Mandy only shook her head.

"But now I think I was wrong."

And before Deacon could utter another breath, Mandy sat herself down beside Jen. When she saw who it was, looking up briefly, Jen's eyes widened and she glanced up to Deacon guiltily.

But he didn't say a word.

Instead, he left them to it, knowing that either way Mandy would not let him interfere.

He was very confused.

He had no idea what was going on.

In fact, he even felt a little betrayed, for though he had sensed there were things Jen and Dyra were keeping from him, he had never imagined they would lead to something like this.

Deacon stepped back out into the hallway and opened the thick, wooden front door to Keepers Cottage, passing through in an instant and once again out into the cold air of the night.

Glancing for a second through the lighted living room window, he could see Dyra talking hurriedly with Mahoney, and Jen shaking as she responded to Mandy's many questions.

By the very word Mandy looked to be growing increasingly worried, and after barely a few moments, Deacon couldn't bear to watch any longer.

His eyes found their way up to the sky, stretching out cold and black and endless above him with a million and more questions still unanswered.

That was exactly how he felt at that moment.

He sighed deeply, and his breath steamed out in warm, white billows above him.

This, whatever it was, was getting out of hand.

But the trouble was, he had fallen for Jen.

There was no question about that.

He couldn't just walk away now.

"Deacon…" A quiet, timid voice sounded from behind him then.

He turned to look, only to find Jen illuminated in the light of the doorway, yearning after him with heavy eyes, and an infinitely heavier heart.

"Jen…" He replied, not knowing what else to say. His voice was hushed to barely a whisper, but it carried through the darkness like an albatross soaring endlessly over the ocean.

"They…I…" She started, struggling with exactly what she wanted to say.

Deacon didn't interrupt.

The time for that was passed.

"I have to…" Jen tried again. "I'm sorry…I have to tell you the truth…" She finally managed.

Though she was trying not to be seen, her efforts were relatively futile, and Deacon could clearly see Mandy glancing worriedly out of the window.

She had tried to make Jen see sense, or at least see reality.

This had gone on long enough.

"Okay…" Deacon replied, still unsure what else he could really say.

"The police want to talk to me…" Jen continued. "Please, will you come with me?"

All of a sudden, Deacon understood what Jen was trying to say.

She was admitting there were things she hadn't told him.

She was asking if he would stay with her if she told him the truth.

She was asking for forgiveness.

Whatever it was, Deacon considered, that Jen had been hiding, he could tell she had been keeping it locked up inside for a long time now. He knew what she was trying to do was very hard for her.

"Of course I will…" He replied, his voice calm and collected as ever.

He had already made his decision, even before she'd asked him the question.

Nonetheless, the relief that surged through Jen in that moment was overwhelmingly obvious.

Following Jen back in, taking her hand as he did so, and interlocking his fingers smoothly with hers, Deacon pulled the door quietly to behind him, keeping what was left of the heat inside.

"Jen…" Officer Mahoney said then, stepping through from the kitchen and walking over to her and Deacon. "How are you feeling?" He asked.

"I'm okay." Jen replied, actually quite assuredly. For one of the first times in almost as long as she could remember, she spoke those words with some semblance of truth.

And actually, Deacon noted, surprisingly, she did look a lot better.

"Good." Mahoney replied gladly. "I've spoken to your mother about what's happened." He explained, and Jen nodded. "I will need your two's accounts…" He went on, and Jen and Deacon both nodded again in agreement.

"That's fine." Jen confirmed.

"We won't do it all now." Mahoney assured them. "We have a pretty good idea already. There's just one thing I need for now…" He pressed, though quite gently, glancing briefly at Deacon as he spoke.

Both of them caught on to his meaning, but this time Jen was quick to intervene.

"That's fine." She asserted, reaching up with her free hand to clutch Deacon's arm, signifying with that single gesture much more than she could have done with all her words.

"Okay…" Mahoney agreed, though admittedly a little warily. "Was it definitely him?" He asked Jen, looking her dead in the eyes as he spoke.

"Yes." She replied in an instant.

"You're sure?" He asked, but Jen did not budge.

"Definitely." She confirmed. "I'm sure."

"Very well then…" Mahoney concluded, making a quick note in a small, black notebook. "Thank you. In that case, I'll leave you two to it…" His voice trailed off slightly, but his eyes betrayed the fact that clearly he was not envious of what Jen now had to do.

He smiled somewhat half-heartedly and bade them goodnight.

Deacon, however, following that final remark, was much more nervous than he had been before.

When Jen turned to him and beckoned him to follow her upstairs, he swallowed hard as they slowly ascended the rickety staircase, up and into yet more darkness.

Truth

It was a cold night, true, but atop the rooftop of Keepers Cottage, on sea view side, the air had a harsh, biting chill to it that seemed to set the precedent of the evening quite accurately.

Dragging her quilt up and out of the window with them, Jen and Deacon settled upon the rooftop, tucking the blanket around each other and cocooning themselves together in a nest of safety and warmth.

At first they did not speak.

Jen leant back against Deacon's chest, feeling his heat and his strong heartbeat protecting her from the suffocating cold all around. He draped his arms over her front and she clung to his hands as if she were afraid to ever let him go.

Sat like this, after the madness of the evening, it wasn't long before tears rolled openly down Jen's face, warming her cheeks in wet streaks as they went.

Hushing her gently, Deacon managed to quiet her swelling sadness, but he didn't want to push her too much, for he knew there was still much more to come.

Behind the house trees rustled and swayed in the blackness as the wind picked up slightly and whipped about their cocoon. Jen sunk deeper into Deacon and he pulled her ever closer, enveloping her securely, as he always did.

"I've got a problem…" Jen suddenly confessed, her voice slicing through the night like a sharpened blade.

Albatross

"Can I help?" Deacon asked after a moment.

"You're the only one who's made any difference at all." Jen told him, but her words only confused Deacon further.

"I don't understand." He admittedly honestly. "I haven't done anything."

But Jen shook her head.

"You have." She replied adamantly. "You're the only one who has."

"What about your mother and your sister?" Deacon asked then.

Even as he spoke he felt Jen's body tense slightly, but he pressed on.

"I've known you barely a month…" He continued. "If this has been going on a while, whatever it is, haven't they been able to help?"

"They can't." Jen replied immediately, but Deacon refused to accept that as gospel.

"They must be able to do something? If not Dyra, then what about Clare?" He suggested. "I can see how much you love her, even just in the pictures downstairs. I know how close you two are…"

But Jen cut him off.

"Were…"

"What?" Deacon asked, confused again.

"How close we were…" Jen finished, sighing deeply and regretfully.

Now Deacon thought he was beginning to understand.

"So, this problem…" He started. "It's with Clare…"

Jen didn't reply, and so Deacon took that silence as a profound yes.

"Right…" He continued, pretty much just thinking aloud. "So, what happened that pushed you so far apart?"

"It wasn't her fault…" Jen whispered, her voice lost almost entirely to the wind.

"Did you do something?" Deacon asked her.

His question was not accusing; he just needed to know.

"I couldn't…" Jen croaked, tears welling up again. "I wanted to…"

"Wanted to what?" Deacon pressed gently.

"I wanted to help!" Jen exclaimed, shuddering and shaking suddenly as grief overwhelmed her. "I couldn't!" She cried. "I should have…I could have…"

Deacon pulled her close and quieted her, resting his palm against her cheek tenderly.

"I'm sorry…I'm sorry…I'm sorry…" Jen apologised, repeating it over and over and over again, whiling her breath away as she spoke.

Deacon couldn't tell if she was apologising to him, or whether it was for something else entirely, and he got the impression, actually, that it was a little of both.

"Shh…" He calmed her. "It's okay…" He did his best to reassure her.

"I should have told you…" Jen confessed, looking up at him through the dim light.

He leaned forward to kiss her, wiping the streaming tears from her cheeks and pressing his warm lips to hers.

"It's okay…" He assured her again. "Whatever it is, it'll be okay. I still love you…"

Albatross

Jen looked on at Deacon, overwhelmed by his kindness, and he looked back expectantly, though clearly, and understandably so, nervously.

Opening her mouth to speak again, Jen croaked a little and struggled to talk, partly because of the state she was in, and partly because she just couldn't find the right words.

It was as if the very thing she needed to tell him, she was still trying to convince herself was true.

She didn't want to believe it either.

Deacon sighed.

Sometimes his perception was just as much a curse as it was a gift, especially when something eluded him.

He rested his hand gently on Jen's cheek again, and looked into her eyes with his all-seeing gaze.

His trust in her was obvious, and it seemed to give Jen courage.

Once again, it was now or never.

She took another breath, still drawn entirely by his gaze, and took the leap.

"Deacon…" Jen whispered into the night, for a second time shattering the silence of the darkness all around them with her words.

"I'm here…" He breathed back at her through the blackness, and Jen nodded slowly, holding back a scream that she had kept hidden within for a very long time.

"Clare's dead."

Revelations

Unsurprisingly, that night, Jen's dreams were not peaceful. They were wild and treacherous and yet again plagued by a haunted past. The dark of the night once more took her on a long, sinister trip down Memoria Lane, stirring the darkest thoughts and emotions from deep within her.

The blackness loomed upon her menacingly and, compared the other dreams she'd had of late, this one felt much more like a memory, like a reality even, than just simply a subconscious fiction.

The lane stretched out limitlessly in both directions, shrouding all that Jen could see in darkness, and everything remained hidden from her.

A hint of devious, low hanging fog that she hadn't noticed before brushed coldly against Jen's face, wet to the touch.

There was no wind that she could feel, yet all about her the trees swayed and bowed this way and that, bending their wills obediently. Their huge looming trunks concealed much of the light from the streetlamps, dotted haphazardly along the lane, and beyond them the bushes and shrubs were shrouded in almost total blackness.

Jen knew that at one end of the lane lay the shop where Clare worked.

She rounded the corner that once again appeared from nowhere, and continued towards it, presuming that somewhere along the way she would bump into her older sister.

Albatross

Checking her watch, Jen knew that Clare had already finished, for it was long past the hour, and the shop would be closed at this time. Surely she would be on her way by now.

But, as she peered into the distance through the dim light and the thickening fog, Jen could see no sign of Clare.

Suddenly a noise off to the side of the road startled her. It was a sound that she recognised all too well, but it still caught her off guard, and fear of the unknown began racing through her veins.

This time though, she didn't call immediately for help, and took a few tentative steps towards the treeline, squinting to try to make out any shapes in the darkness.

She wasn't far from a streetlamp, but ironically, if anything, that only hindered her view, for it cast yet more shadows onto the greenery beneath the trees.

Creeping forward, keeping as silent as she could, Jen edged closer and closer, stepping from the tarmacked road and onto the soft verge beyond, squatting down low and peering through the trees.

The cry sounded again, this time much closer, and much louder, and much more desperate.

And above all else, it sounded like Clare calling her name.

Jen's lungs drove into action.

"Help!" She cried. "Is anybody there!?"

But no one came to her aid.

Then, just as she recalled from her last dream, a figure appeared from the shadows, separating itself from the blackness and the shadows as if it belonged to them.

This might have been a dream, but it was no fairy tale fiction, and Jen knew it.

No matter how much she might not have wanted it to be, this was a memory, and she had absolutely no choice in the matter.

With that knowledge, as she crouched, transfixed for barely a few seconds by the shadowy figure before her, Jen was gripped by fear.

All of a sudden the figure darted away between the trees, skirting round Jen and exploding from the treeline and out onto the road, sprinting off into the distance at full pelt.

He was dressed all in black, from his boots to his jacket, and he glanced back only once as he raced away, catching Jen's eye as he did so by the light of the nearest streetlamp.

Her breath caught in her throat at the sight.

It was him.

The man who had broken into Keepers Cottage and tried to kill Deacon to get to her.

His hair was a little shorter, a little less unkempt and dishevelled, but it was most definitely him.

Jen didn't have time to think on that however, as the faint cry sounded once more from beyond the treeline, and this time, following her own shout for help, there was a much more discernible word amongst the sound.

"Jenny…"

The voice was weak and desperate, clinging to faint hope, but it was one that Jen knew all too well.

Without thinking, stumbling blindly forwards, Jen hit her head on low branches three times before she pulled her phone from her pocket and fumbled to turn on the torch.

Finally she found it, and immediately the light shone just over the bush directly before her, and beyond it the sight than Jen beheld turned her stomach.

"NO!!" She screamed, diving immediately down through the shrubbery and to the side of the figure that lay on the cold, damp ground.

In an instant she felt her hands and knees turn sticky and warm, as she knelt on the ground by torchlight.

"No…" Jen's voice weakened, overwhelmed. "No no no no…"

"Jenny…" Clare breathed, weakening more and more by the second, coughing up blood and spluttering as she spoke, choking and gargling.

The word seemed more like a reflex than a cry for help, and Jen looked on helplessly.

Her sister's trousers and underwear were pulled down to her ankles. Her jacket and blouse were ripped open and soaked in blood, showing her pale, exposed skin beneath, sticky and black and oozing from a gash in her stomach.

Lying beside her head was a large rock, smothered too in thick, black gunk. Blood poured from a battered hole in Clare's skull, seeping through her hair until it was completely drenched in it.

"Clare…" Jen words caught in her throat.

She tried to call for help, but she could not speak: paralysed by fear and shock.

But then Clare spluttered and gargled again, choking up vast amounts of blood as she tried to talk.

Jen found her tongue.

"HELP!!" She shrieked deafeningly. "SOMEONE HELP!!" Even as she screamed she dialled for an ambulance and bellowed almost incoherently down the phone at the operator.

Descending into the deepest depths of the blackness, there was simply nothing else Jen could do.

She tried to stop the bleeding, but Clare's head was gaping, and there was so much blood pumping out of her stomach that Jen couldn't even see the wound.

She just held her older sister's hand as blood poured over them both, covering them in all that was left of Clare's life.

Drowning and gasping, it wasn't long before Clare succumbed, but every second was agony for them both, and Jen wailed and screeched and shrieked.

She couldn't live without Clare.

She didn't know how.

But from that moment on, regardless of whether she wanted it or not, there was a great cavernous void inside of Jen that could never again be filled.

Startling awake, Jen screamed, shaking and bawling in agony and grief.

Deacon was there of course, but for now at least, there was only so much he could do.

Albatross

So far, time hadn't been the greatest of healers.

But, as it stood, that was all that they had.

That's all anybody ever has.

Some people go their entire lives thinking that void can never be filled.

Perhaps they are right.

Perhaps they are wrong.

Either way, often they put all of their trust in the miraculous healing power of time.

But sometimes, even that isn't enough.

Not when there's a festering thought consuming you.

Just like family though, that great void can mean lots of different things. And what we do with it, what we make of it, can perhaps lead us places that we have never even dreamed of.

Not all of us have the strength to follow such a difficult path.

But, for those who do, and for those who are fortunate enough to have someone to support them along the way, here's to a new life.

Letting Go

Morning did not come quickly, and the darkness tormented Jen cruelly.

She rose early, more so to avoid sleep than out of any real necessity. In his concern, naturally, Deacon accompanied her, and his all-seeing gaze followed her as she swept slowly around the kitchen in a routine so solemn and ingrained that she didn't even need to think about it.

Occasionally Jen glanced across at Deacon sat at the kitchen table, and he smiled at her affectionately. She returned his smile as best she could, but she found it particularly difficult that morning.

Every time, Jen couldn't help but let her gaze drift across to the opposite side of the table, where Clare sat. Watching her younger sister, her eyes were filled with sadness and regret, as they so often had been these past twelve months.

"You okay?" Deacon asked softly, seeing Jen glance across to the empty seat opposite him for the fifth time.

"Yeah…" Jen lied, unconvincingly, as she laid out four plates upon the worktop for breakfast.

Deacon raised his eyebrows slightly, but didn't say a word. After a moment of silence, realising all of a sudden what she'd done, Jen sighed deeply and sorrowfully, and placed one plate back into the cupboard, closing the door silently.

Jen panned bacon and eggs together, sliced tomatoes and grilled them, toasted bread until it was crisp and buttered it smoothly, all with a well-practiced hand. But her mind was not on food, and she wasn't hungry in the slightest.

Finally, giving up, she groaned and placed down everything she was holding, leaning her elbows down onto the worktop and dropping her head into her hands.

"I can't do this anymore…" She sighed, and in an instant Deacon was there beside her.

"You can do it." He tried to reassure her. "It'll be alright…"

But Jen just shook her head in denial.

Though, saying that, she had been in denial for quite some time now.

And even Deacon struggled to believe his own words, now that he knew the truth, and he glanced around the kitchen as if he expected there to be somebody else there with them.

Clare was still sat at the table, and she looked on at him with an expression painted across her face that was a mixture of so many different emotions it was all but unreadable.

Jen wrenched her head from her hands and looked across at her.

Her older sister's expression changed and she smiled, her eyes comforting and understanding.

Finally making her decision, Jen's mind was all of a sudden set.

"Deacon…" She started, and he looked back to her yearningly.

"Yes?" He asked.

"I have to show you something…" She told him, and as she did so she glanced across once again at Clare.

Her sister's face dropped dramatically, as if Jen had just delivered the killing blow herself. Guilt ripped through Jen's veins at the sight, but, in the end, she held firm, knowing at long last what she had to do.

"Okay." Deacon agreed, not knowing what it was that Jen wanted to show him, but getting the impression it would be of monumental importance.

Without another word, hearing the sound of faint footsteps above them, Jen began plating up their breakfast.

Clare rose slowly and rather ominously from her seat, passing Deacon as she walked over to Jen.

He felt a shiver run up and down his spine at her gaze, but, of course, he had no idea what caused it.

"You can't…" Clare whispered urgently to her younger sister. "You know you don't want to…"

Jen nodded, knowing of course that Clare was right.

But this time, at long last, she could see reality more clearly. She knew now that, sadly, she had no other choice.

This was just what she had to do.

Clare nodded, in the end understanding as well, but tears stood heavily in her eyes, and she longed to hold her sister, to put her arm around her and tell her everything was going to be alright.

But, just as had been the case for almost a year now, she knew she couldn't.

And perhaps simply that knowledge, more profound than the hundreds of other reasons, was why Jen had to finally let her go.

The morning was crisp and cold.

Fallen leaves whipped up off the ground in great flurries, swarming around the two of them as Jen and Deacon, hand in hand, paced down the narrow lanes.

Where Jen was leading him exactly, Deacon didn't know, but he felt not the need to ask.

All the while, keeping a steady, level pace with the young couple, Clare remained.

Jen wore a thick hoody to keep the chill wind at bay, and Deacon wore his rugged jacket, for indeed the air was harsh.

As usual, Clare felt not the cold, and wore a plain, red dress that thrashed about her bare, flawless legs wildly.

Turning down a rough track then, one which Deacon had never before followed, Jen led him further and further past the treeline. The ground here was rocky and bumpy, and had clearly not been repaved for quite a few years.

Trees leaned in to grab them as they walked by, reaching over and down towards them yearningly. But when Clare swept by, all but unnoticed, they ignored her presence entirely, just as most did nowadays.

A tall set of black iron gates emerged ahead of them from between the trees, looming high and menacing in their path. Set deep into the ground beside them was a large, brick cenotaph, and upon it was bolted a bronzed plaque, worn and faded by the torturous passage of time.

Cemetery Drive

All of a sudden Deacon understood.

Jen glanced up at him with a wry smile upon her face, knowing there was no turning back now.

He stepped up to the huge gate and pulled the rusty iron bolt across that kept it closed against the wind. With an eerie creak he pulled one of them ajar so that Jen could slip through, and once she had, he followed, closing and bolting it behind them, leaving Clare stood outside gazing after them.

Jen steered Deacon through the oceanic maze of headstones.

Some were small and quite faded, with only very short inscriptions engraved upon them. Whilst others, enormous and towering, had giant sarcophagus bases and huge crosses that drove up towards the sky regally.

Finally, as they swam through the sea of graves, Jen brought them to a stop, and they began to slowly tread water.

Before them lay a single, grey headstone, relatively new compared to many of the others around it, and only just beginning to show the wear and tear of time.

Upon it was engraved but a few lines, the text plain and black and unmarked.

Albatross

Clare Williams

23rd of March, 1996 - 10th of October 2014

Taken from us too soon

Forever in our hearts

And there, stood upon the grave, though not for all to see, was Clare, gazing at her younger sister once more with heavy eyes, but an indescribably heavier heart.

"I'm sorry, Jen..." Deacon breathed, not knowing what else to say.

She didn't reply.

Instead, she just wrapped her arms tightly around him and he embraced her back, sharing his warmth with her on that bitter day.

Jen shuddered as she took a deep breath, gazing with her head rested upon Deacon's chest at Clare. Her older sister, beautiful in her plain red dress, hands clasped together in front of her, stood upon her own grave as if all of this was just as bad dream.

But the look in Clare's eyes confirmed brutally for Jen, for the last time, that this was no nightmare.

It was far too real to imagine such a thing.

"I don't know if I can take this..." Jen whispered, talking to Clare just as much as she was talking to Deacon.

Deacon held her ever tighter, and Clare just pursed her lips and shook her head.

Neither of them could say nor do anything that would ease Jen's suffering.

Only she could do what needed to be done, and that just made it harder.

"I'll always be here…" Deacon finally breathed in reply, and Jen knew he was telling her the truth.

His words comforted her, a little at least.

Then, when he spoke again, for he could see that Jen was looking over at something, though of course he couldn't see what, he sighed deeply.

"Is Clare here too?" He whispered.

In response, clasping her hand about his and interlocking their fingers, Jen began walking slowly away from the grave.

Clare didn't move, and Jen knew she wouldn't follow.

Not anymore.

Jen turned to look back, once and only once.

A single tear escaped her grasp and cascaded down her cheek, streaking warmth everywhere it went upon her cold face. She looked up and Deacon with brimming eyes, before looking back over to her sister, Clare, and took a deep, shuddering breath.

"No…" She finally breathed in reply, her voice thick with emotion.

And within an instant, where Clare had just stood upon her own grave, only a moment ago, now it was empty, and Jen's older sister was nowhere to be seen.

Jen gazed at her sister's headstone, all alone, cast into sudden shadow as a lone cloud drifted across the sky and blocked out the sun.

And Clare was gone.

Forever.

"She's never been here…" Jen whispered, throwing her quiet words onto the wind that wasn't there.

Squeezing Deacon's hand tightly as she looked back up to him, Jen's eyes were filled with immeasurable grief.

And so, without another word that need be said, between the endless seas of headstones the two of them departed.

Side by side, hand in hand, off into the new day they ventured.

Ross Turner

Thank you for reading Albatross

I hope you enjoyed it

If you did then you may also enjoy:

The Redwoods - Book One

Young Vivian Featherstone comes from a long line of Lords and Ladies, and her family's seat of unquestionable influence, wealth and power is owed to a much treasured heirloom, passed down from generation to generation.

But when little Vivian, only eleven years of age, narrowly escapes a plot by a rival, feuding family to eliminate the Featherstones, she finds herself lost in the mysterious Redwood Forest.

With assassins pursuing her, and strange and dangerous creatures all around, can Vivian survive? And will she discover the power of her family's heirloom before it's too late?

The Redwoods Rise and Fall - Book Two

Vivian has returned to Virtus, she has defeated the Greystones, and the once great city even seems to be well on the way to recovery. But something isn't right. Vivian feels stranded amongst all that she has fought to gain, and suffered so terribly to lose. And now it seems there are new threats and dangers, stemming from old evils. Just as all those before her have either succeeded or succumbed, now she too must face her own rise and fall.

Ross Turner

Or

Voices in the Mirror

Evening encroached upon them and a deep, vast, endless darkness swept in upon the tiny, insignificant village of Riverbrook.

Cold winds cut through the trees and bit harshly at the exposed faces of anybody who dared still remain out under the enormous sky, scattered with an ocean of burned out stars that seethed and watched without a sound.

A million and more shining eyes that had gazed down upon the face of the Earth for a hundred millennia and even longer, turned their cruel eyes now to all that was unfolding before them, and for not the first time in history, something impossible and wonderful, a miracle, began to unfold.

Please visit my facebook and twitter pages for the latest updates

Ross Turner Books
@RossTurnerBooks

www.rossturnerbooks.net

Printed in Great Britain
by Amazon